Holy ReVenge

A NOVEL BY

JESSICA A. ROBINSON

Author of *Holy Seduction*

*From the Author of Holy Seduction
and Pretty Skeletons*

ISBN-13: 978-0-9850763-2-0

PEACE IN THE STORM PUBLISHING, LLC.
P.O. Box 1152
Pocono Summit, PA 18346

Visit our Web site at www.PeaceInTheStormPublishing.com

HOLY REVENGE

A NOVEL BY
JESSICA A. ROBINSON

PEACE IN THE STORM PUBLISHING, LLC

Acknowledgements

Wow, I can't believe I'm on book number three already! God has been so good, and I'm so thankful for Him trusting me with such an awesome gift. He continues to amaze me, and I'm so fortunate to be able to do the very thing that I love. Thank you Lord, for all my many blessings, I never want to take them or You for granted.

To my wonderful family, there are no words to express how much I love you and appreciate you. Thanks for always standing beside me, and behind me, as I travel toward my destiny. As always, special thanks to my brothers; Michael and Gabriel Robinson. It's been great watching you two continue to grow and be blessed with the tools to take over the world. I love you both very much.

To Terrence J. Miles; thanks for being such an awesome addition to my life. I appreciate you for everything you've done. Love you. Peanut Butter and Jelly, remember? (Smile)

My Everlife Church family is the best family to have in the whole wide world! Thanks for always being the first ones to support everything I do. I am so lucky to have you in my life. To all my friends know that I love and appreciate you all.

Special thanks to my writing buddy: Julia "Press" Simmons who has truly been a God-send during the writing of this novel. Thanks for reading everything and giving me your honest feedback. It is greatly appreciated and I was glad to be able to do the same for you!

Special thanks to Yolanda L. Gore (my sister ☺), Olivia Stith, and Roslyn Winfield. I also would like to thank Mike Forney and Hot Topix Book Club. Thanks for all your support.

I would like to thank my wonderful publisher Elissa Gabrielle and Peace in the Storm Publishing for believing in me. Thank you for everything.

To anyone else whom I didn't mention just know that I love and appreciate everything you have done for me. I thank you from the bottom of my heart.

Dedication

This book is dedicated to Shannon B. Robinson, aka Nanny. I love you with all my heart and I miss you so much. You pressed on through hard times in your life and just watching your life has forever changed mine. I will never forget the impact you've had on my life and the lives of others around you. You were not only my cousin, but you were and always will be my sister. I will never forget the great times we spent together, all the laughs, and even though you're not here with me physically, I carry you around in my heart everywhere I go. You will always be my angel, I love you.

Staring through the barrel of that chrome gun has definitely changed my life forever. It has caused me not to play the games that I used to play. Rather, it has caused me to find a smarter way to play.

~Denise Tate, aka, The First Lady~

MY THOUGHTS

You would think that ever since my crazed, ex-lover/baby daddy Tyrone busted up in my husband's church toting a loaded gun and trying to kill me, that it would've been the wake-up call that I needed to finally get my act together; but I guess you can say I'm a little hardheaded. My mother always used to say I was hardheaded as a child. And you know what they say about hard heads: **A hard head makes a soft BEHIND...**

PROLOGUE

"This all feels like a bad dream, it doesn't even seem real." I kicked off my black, *Christian Louboutin* heels, and shut the door after Terri walked in carrying Kaylah in her car seat.

"Yeah it doesn't feel real at all." Terri replied, and bent down to pick up Kaylah out of her car seat but I motioned for her to leave her right where she was.

"Please let that little girl sleep, she's been crying a lot lately and hasn't really slept all week."

"For real?"

"I think she can feel what's going on around her."

"You think so? I don't think she does, but I do know that babies pick up when there's stress in their environment." Terri replied, as I carried the car seat into the living room and we sat down on the couch.

"Maybe that's what it is because she's been a little insomniac lately." I bent down and removed Kaylah's coat without waking her at all.

I don't know why my daughter has been all fussy lately. But whatever has her this upset is not good at all. I swear if I smoked weed I'd be rolling up a fat one right now. For weeks, she hasn't slept the entire night through. No matter if she's fed and dry, she still cries and I've taken her to the doctor and she's perfectly fine. She must know what's going on even though she's not old enough to understand anything.

"It's hard to believe that Tyrone is gone."

"I've been trying to wrap my mind around it all week but I can't." Denise said.

"That's just crazy how everything went down. I couldn't believe he had the nerve to bust up in church and go off like that in the middle of service the way he did."

"I know, it sounds like a scene straight out of the movies." My mind quickly recalled the moment in the church when Tyrone burst into Oakdale like a crazy man. Although I was ashamed at his antics that day, it did play out just like a scene from a real movie, except there was no director to yell, 'cut' and at the end of the day a life was gone.

"I tell you one thing, I'm glad that Deacon Russell still carries his gun, otherwise you might not even be here." Terri lightly touched my arm and then looked off in the opposite direction. Just her slight touch caused me to have goose bumps. I know what she was saying was the honest to God truth, but it still produced an eerie feeling when she actually said it out loud.

"That was nothing but God watching over me." I replied.

I blinked my eyes several times trying to rid my mind of what could've happened if Deacon Russell hadn't stopped Tyrone. My mind couldn't even fathom not being around to be a mother to my child, or a wife to my husband. I tried my best not to think about the 'what ifs'. I was just grateful to be alive at that point. I counted my blessings knowing that God had spared my life for a reason, and Tyrone's death proved to be the wake-up call that I needed to get my life back together. I looked at it as my personal confirmation to get myself right and rid my life of all of the unnecessary junk that resided in my world. From this point on, my main concerns were with being a great wife and a great mother.

"Where's Randy at? I thought he would've made it home by now." Terri asked, as she glanced down at her *Rolex* watch.

"Oh, he should be home soon. He said he had a few things to finish up at the church after the funeral. He should be coming home shortly." I explained. I actually felt blessed to even say he was on his way home. After all I did, I thought he would've kicked me to the curb; but thank God for His mercy.

"I really respect Randy for still giving that jerk a funeral at our church after what he tried to do to you." Terri raised her eyebrows and scrunched her face.

"Shoot, I respect him too. If that had been my decision to make, I would've put that fool in a pine box and called it a day with his crazy behind; but you know my Randy, he believed since he was still a member of Oakdale, then he deserved a proper home going service."

"Wow, like I said, I have a new-found respect for him. If you didn't know already, that man loves you girl. I don't know too many men who would've done that."

I shook my head in agreement with Terri because I knew she was speaking the truth. There weren't many men who would stay with their wife after they found out that she not only cheated on them behind their back, but she had also conceived a child with that man too. I also didn't know of too many men that would choose to stay and love their wife after all of that; so for that very reason alone, I was thankful to have a man like Randy in my life.

Just as I was going to say something else, I heard the garage door lifting up which meant Randy was pulling his Cadillac Escalade into his usual parking space right next to mine. Terri's phone began to ring and she smiled before answering it. I looked at my best friend a little strange because I've never seen her smile like that when someone called her.

"Hey you." Terri smiled again and pressed the phone closer in her ear. I giggled as I watched my best friend converse with whoever she was talking to like she was a high school kid again. Kaylah begin to stir in her car seat enough to where I decided to pick her up. I cradled her in my arms thinking that she was trying to wake up, but surprisingly, she worked herself back into a deep sleep. I walked across the room and placed her on the love seat on her back.

"So who's the lucky man that has you blushing like a school girl?" I asked as I saw Terri had ended her phone call.

"That was Carlos." Terri answered, and pressed her lips together blushing.

"Carlos?" I tried to jog my memory, but his name didn't ring a bell.

"I've told you about him. I met him last month. Remember, I told you we met downtown while I was having a business lunch at *Rosetta Stone*."

"Oh, yeah, the guy that's an architect; right?" I remembered.

"Yes, that's him." Terri smiled.

"Well, I don't know what he's done to you, but it has to obviously be something special because I've never seen you smile like this before."

"We've been seeing each other since last month, and everything is going good so far; he just called because he wants to take me to dinner tonight; so that's where I'm going." Terri said, as she got up from the couch, walked over to the love seat, and kissed Kaylah on her cheek.

"Where is he going to take you?"

"I don't know. He says it's a surprise and our dates seem to be getting better and better, so I can only imagine. I'll see ya later. Hey Randy!" Terri turned around and saw him standing in the archway of the living room.

"Hey Terri, it's good to see you." He walked over and gave her a quick hug and she walked through the foyer and out the front door.

"Hey babe, I'm glad you made it home so fast. I thought you would've been at the church till later this evening." I got up from my seat and walked over to where he was standing. I wrapped my arms around his neck and kissed him on his lips.

"Surprisingly, I didn't have as much work as I anticipated. Where's my baby at?" Randy asked as he looked at her empty car seat. I pulled away and pointed in the direction of the couch.

"There's Sleeping Beauty."

"She was acting like she wanted to wake up a little while ago, but I guess she still isn't done taking her nap."

"That's what babies do best, I'm glad she's sleeping good now. That way we can get some sleep too." Randy loosened his tie from around his neck and slipped it off.

"Well, since Kaylah is still sleep, I thought it would give you and me a chance to do some relaxing of our own." I winked, and then put my arms around his neck again. He attempted to say something, but I placed my French-manicured finger up to his lip to stop him. I wasn't in the mood to hear any excuses as to why he wasn't up for making love. I just wanted to be intimate with him right then and there. I began to kiss him on the lips and then traveled down to his neck. I unbuttoned his white dress shirt and started to run my fingers up and down his washboard abs. I could tell he enjoyed what I was doing to him because he closed his eyes and titled his head back; taking everything in.

I went a step further and undid his belt buckle and in almost an instant, Randy snapped out of the seductive trance that I was trying to put him in.

"Not now honey. I'm tired. I just want to relax." Randy fastened his belt buckle back to its original position. I looked at my husband with a confused look on my face. *Talk about mixed signals.*

"Well, I can help you to relax if you just let me." I smiled, as I leaned in to kiss him, but he moved away from me causing me to stumble slightly.

"Honey, that's okay. It's been a long day. I'm about to go to the den for a while, come and bring Kaylah to me when she wakes up; ok?" Randy bent down, kissed me on my forehead, and was on his way

HOLY REVENGE

down the hallway before I could even speak a word of protest.

I stared down the vacant hallway and then over in the living room toward our daughter who was still sleeping.

Did my husband just do what I think he did? Yup, he just denied me sex. Wow!

He had denied me a few times during this whole Tyrone ordeal, but I hoped this wasn't becoming a routine between us. I knew it might take a little while for *that* part of our marriage to be restored, but I prayed that this was only a season and one that didn't last very long. There was a part of me that wanted to be frustrated with the way he was choosing to act, but I quickly shook off my feelings. The road to repairing our marriage was not going to be an easy one, and since my husband decided to remain in our relationship and not head for divorce court, I figured I would do what I had to do until times got better. Because God had not only spared my life and my marriage; but I had also promised God that I would put an end to my wild ways. No more engaging in relationships with other men. I made a decision to give all those things up in order to be the wife that Randy deserved to have.

I knew that it would take time to get our relationship back to where it needed to be, but I was willing to do whatever I had to do in order to help us get back to a good place. I was just thankful to still be married to Randy, and I figured things would heal themselves and get better in time. As long as I remained a perfect wife, then Randy would have no choice but to return back to how things used to be.

Chapter 1 (Denise)

"**I**f you need to reach me for any reason, you have me and my husband's cell phone numbers. I should be back early this afternoon." I handed Kaylah to Marisol who was our personal housekeeper, nanny, and a true God-send. Kaylah began to laugh and talk as Marisol called her name. I was relieved that my daughter took so well to Marisol, because it gave me the freedom to come and go as I pleased. Some women feel that you're a bad mother if you hire a nanny, but I beg to differ. I feel like the mothers who choose to hire nannies are just that much smarter.

"Okay Mrs. Tate, if I need anything, I'll call you right away." She replied in her thick Spanish accent. I simply smiled. It was great to have a person who not only watched my child, but who could also cook up some Spanish rice and beans too upon request. It was the best feeling in the world.

"Marisol, I know you're trying to be professional and everything, but please call me Denise." I reminded her.

"Okay Denise." She replied. I kissed Kaylah on her cheek and then walked out the door.

I never thought I would see the day that I would need to hire someone to help me around the house, but being the wife of a prominent pastor, and now a new mother, proved to be more challenging than ever. I thought that I'd be able to keep up with the busy demands of my eight-month-old daughter, plus cook and clean our six thousand square-foot home, but after a few months it was hard to stay on top of it all. Not to mention that I had started becoming more involved with things over at Oakdale. So when I came across Marisol's personal ad in *The Vindicator* two months ago, she had truly been a God-send to me.

I drove my red Mercedes Benz down the street and through our neighborhood. The warm June air swept through the car in a breeze, and I had to smile because I absolutely loved this time of year. I could hear the birds chirping and singing their own melody as I drove in the direction of the church. I looked at all the children who were playing in their own yards, and I couldn't help but think of Kaylah. I couldn't wait until my daughter was old enough to play outside with other kids. Since the weather had been so warm lately, I made a mental note to take her to the park soon.

After ten minutes into my drive, I called Randy's office number but he didn't answer. I immediately hung up and dialed his cell phone number and it went directly to voicemail.

That's not like him to not answer any of his phones.

I knew he was in a bad mood when I called him this morning. I could tell it from the sound of his voice. But he claimed that everything was fine. There was something in his tone that suggested he wasn't being truthful, so I decided to take matters into my own hands and have lunch delivered to the church. I figured the surprise visit would be just the trick to lift his spirits.

My cell phone rang before I could even put it back inside my purse. I glanced at the unknown number and then pressed ignore. This was the third time in the past week that someone had called my phone with a number that I didn't recognize. I hoped it wasn't someone trying to play on my phone again, because this time around I would definitely change my number.

Jessica A. Robinson

Shortly after Tyrone died, I'd begun receiving prank calls. Once the news reporters got wind of the fact that a man had been shot and killed inside our church, my phone had been ringing off the hook. I found it quite odd that so many "strangers" had access to my cell phone number which was private; but with the age of the internet I figured anything was possible. I received calls from people who didn't hesitate in telling me how low down, dirty, and trifling I was, and who called me every name in the book but a child of God. These calls started occurring repeatedly to the point that I couldn't even leave my phone on. Finally after three weeks of nonstop verbal slander, I decided to tell my husband about what was going on. He was furious to find out that someone had been harassing me, and he came up with the idea that I should change my number, but I initially decided against it. I just prayed that the string of new phone calls weren't a continuation of the foolishness that I had to experience since Tyrone's death.

I pulled my car into the parking lot of the church and was surprised to only see a few cars there. I parked next to my husband's Cadillac which was parked in its assigned spot. On any given day I'm used to seeing fifteen to twenty cars outside of Oakdale, and there are usually all kinds of people coming in and out of the building, but times had definitely changed since the Sunday that Tyrone had busted up in the church acting like a mad man. After that episode, Randy cut down on all of the people who were allowed access to the church during the day. He felt that it was safer to limit the amount of people who passed in and out the church. I didn't blame him for doing that at all. Just seeing how Tyrone had acted a complete fool was evidence to me that crazy people were more prevalent now than ever.

I turned my car off and pulled the key out of the ignition. Before I got out, I flipped down the visor and checked my appearance in the mirror. I had to admit while some women looked worse after they had a child; motherhood had done wonders for me. Even though I already considered myself to be gorgeous, I could now thank Kaylah for the extra glow that made me appear to be a flawless beauty. My hair had grown out to my chin and I had my hair stylist cut it into a choppy, multi-layered bob, which made me appear more like a runway model than a first lady. Some pastor's wives looked so plain and homely, but not me. That was just not my style. I believed in looking absolutely fabulous. Who said first ladies couldn't be fly? My skin had a luster as if I'd just vacationed on South Beach, and my body was even shapelier than it was before I had the baby. I knew I was a breathtaking beauty, and even though I'd definitely made some major mistakes in my marriage, I knew I was still a catch to any man for sure.

When I walked in the side door, I could smell the delicious pasta that I had ordered from *Antone's* in the air, which meant that they must've just delivered it. I followed the scent up the steps and right past the security desk where Kenny was sitting preoccupied with his phone. He was the last person on earth I wanted to see, but I knew I couldn't avoid him no matter how hard I tried. I intended to walk straight past him, and wished that he was so caught up with what he was doing on his phone, that he wouldn't notice me but that wasn't the case. He wasn't going to let me do that at all. He cleared his throat which caused me to stop and quickly roll my eyes because of the interruption.

"So you're just gonna walk past me like I wasn't sitting here at all?" He asked, as he walked around his desk and leaned against it. I sighed and then rolled my eyes again at Kenny.

"Shouldn't you be circling the perimeter, checking for bad guys, making sure this place is secure? I'm quite sure we don't pay you to be on *Facebook* all day." I asked crossing my arms.

"Don't worry about my job, I do that just fine, but there is something else that I would like the opportunity to do if I had the chance." Kenny lowered his voice, bit down on his bottom lip, and winked. I looked down the hallway to make sure no one was coming. I couldn't believe this simple man had the nerve to slide slick comments my way while we were standing right there in the church.

"Don't you go worrying about that...my husband already has that under control." I winked back and then walked away. I strutted my stuff, making sure I switched my hips as I walked. I knew he was watching anyway. It was nothing like seeing a man look at something he couldn't have. The look on his face was priceless. Ever since Kenny had accepted the position as head over the security department, he had been trying to gain my interest but hadn't succeeded. It wasn't that he was ugly because in the looks department he was finer than wine and I had been tempted, on more than one occasion, to take advantage of the fact that he was interested, but I figured him being a part of the church and staff was too close for comfort for me. I had already had enough with Tyrone joining the church and practically becoming my husband's best friend, and wasn't trying to repeat that whole scenario again. I turned around slightly right before I turned the corner and saw him still standing in the same spot. His eyes were glued to me like a piece of paper and I shook my head, smiled, and kept it moving.

Why in the world is this man so fine? I thought to myself and before I could think about anything else, I closed my eyes and said a quick prayer.

Lord, please remove all the impure thoughts I'm having about this sexy man out of my head. In Jesus name, amen.

It had to be a federal offense for a man to be as fine as Kenny was. His muscular build, long dreads which he kept pulled neatly into a ponytail, the dimple in his right cheek that revealed itself when he was

HOLY REVENGE

trying to flirt, and his perfect white smile all tucked into his six-foot-four frame made him almost irresistible. The way he carried himself turned me on, but I was able to forgo his advances. Even though he was fine as age-old wine, I had made the decision to cut everything else off. That was the promise I had made to myself and God; and it hadn't been easy, but at least I was trying. I really didn't know how to resist a man that looked that good, other than to ignore him and be rude. That was the approach I had been using, and for the time being, it seemed to be working.

I approached the receptionist desk and noticed Tanisha was stuffing two heavy text books inside her book bag.

"Hey Tanisha, where are you off to? I thought today was one of your days to be here until four." I said, as she turned around and smiled at me.

"Hey, First Lady. Yeah, that was my schedule last semester, but now I leave early because my classes are different. I won't be here as much." She stated and then looked down at her watch.

"I'm sorry to run, but I have to get to class" Tanisha said as she put her book bag on her shoulders and walked off. I lifted my mini bottle of *Beautiful* which was my favorite scent, and sprayed myself before walking into Randy's office. I opened the large wooden door and found him sitting at his desk with his hands folded praying. I looked over at the food which was sitting on the table still untouched. The noise from the door caused Randy to open up his eyes and smile.

"Hey baby. To what do I owe this honor?" He asked as he got up and met me in the center of the room and kissed me on my lips.

"Well, I thought I would surprise you and bring you something for lunch especially after the way you sounded on the phone this morning." I wrapped my arms around him and kissed him again. My husband's touch still had the ability to melt me like an ice cube on a summer's day.

Jessica A. Robinson

"I know I didn't sound like myself honey. Please forgive me it's just a lot of changes happening at the church and I'm honestly trying to deal with everything the best way I know how."

"What's going on Randy?" I asked as we walked over to the couch and sat down together.

Randy glanced over at me and sighed. "Well, as of this morning I received a letter of resignation from Minister Willis; which was of complete and utter shock because I thought that he would always be a part of this ministry."

"Why did he resign?" I raised my eyebrows confused.

"He said that he felt that God was calling him to another ministry and that his season was up here at Oakdale, but for some reason I don't know if I believe him. His letter really didn't make sense to me at all."

I let out a sigh of relief as I heard Randy explain to me the reason why Minister Willis was resigning and was glad he didn't state the real reason for his sudden resignation. I was glad he made up some bogus explanation as to why he was leaving, rather than explaining to Randy that he'd been trying to secretly get me to sleep with him ever since the church found out I had been unfaithful. I didn't have any problem with resisting him because he wasn't even my type and he looked like a grease ball that enjoyed sleeping with anything considered female.

He wouldn't leave me alone until I got word from another church member that he'd been sleeping with a few underage girls at the school he worked at as a teacher. When I revealed that I knew what he was doing, and if he didn't leave me alone that I would expose him for the jerk he really was, he told me he would be resigning and moving out of town. I didn't know he was really serious about doing so, but to hear that he actually followed through with his alleged plan made me a very happy woman.

HOLY REVENGE

"Well, if he's saying that his season has ended here with us, then we just have to believe he's truly hearing from the Lord and let him go." I said as I rubbed his back. I could feel the knots in his shoulders and knew that he was truly stressing over the issue.

"I understand babe; and you're making perfect sense, but he was a real asset to this ministry. He was the one responsible for starting and maintaining the single's ministry and with him leaving, that is going to create a void for a while until I can find someone who can replace him"

"Don't worry Randy. I'm confident that you will."

Randy sighed and then wiped a few beads of sweat from his brow.

"That's not all."

"You mean someone else has chosen to leave too?" I asked surprised.

"Yeah. it's Tanisha. You know she has been waiting to hear back from the university she applied to so she can go to medical school; well, they just sent her a letter in the mail yesterday. She leaves in two weeks for Georgia."

"That's wonderful. I know she's been waiting a long time to get accepted into that medical school." I smiled.

"She has, but since she's leaving so soon that makes another position that's open and even though she's not a minister heading up a ministry, she's just as important as anyone else to this church. I will need someone full time to fill that position and help keep things around here straight."

"Well, why don't you put the word out in the church and see if someone's interested in taking the position?" I suggested.

"Either way I'm going to have to do something. If not someone in the church, then I'll need to put a personal ad in the newspaper and find someone who's qualified."

Jessica A. Robinson

I sat and pondered everything my husband told me, and then it was as if a light bulb went off in my head.

"Or baby I can always come and be your full-time secretary. I know with me being here it will help you." I replied.

"Honey, I can't ask you to do that. You already have enough with Kaylah and doing things around the house. I think that would be too much for you." Randy said as I shook my head 'no'.

"No, it'll be fine, besides with Marisol helping out around the house and taking care of the baby, it gives me more free time; so why not come in and help you out. It would be my pleasure." I smiled. Randy breathed a sigh of relief and then hugged me.

"Wow. You don't know how much this is gonna help me out. I really appreciate you doing this. It's a lot of work, but I know you can handle it." Randy kissed me softly.

"Oh, I can handle it. Once the women's conference is over, I'll be here to fill Tanisha's spot. Now listen, let's go over to the table and have lunch before our food gets cold; everything else will work itself out. Trust me." I went to get up from the couch and walk toward where our food was, but Randy grabbed me by the hand.

"Denise, I just want you to know that I appreciate all of the hard work you've been putting in coordinating the women's conference and everything else you've been doing to assist me. I know we've been through some rough times, and still go through our moments, but I love you and I'm so glad you're my wife."

"Thank you baby. I love you too. Thank you for being such a wonderful husband to me and father to our daughter. I'm so blessed to have a man like you in my life and I promise that I will continue to do what I can to be a blessing to you."

HOLY REVENGE

Randy pulled me in close to him and I stood motionless inhaling his scent. I couldn't deny the fact that I loved this man and he loved me too. I felt as though I was in heaven and floating on the clouds, and honestly, I didn't want the feeling to end. I was glad Randy was starting to be more loving and affectionate toward me like he used to.

I missed the way he used to just hold me without having to say a word. Or the way he would look into my eyes with such love and adoration. I missed the ways we would be intimate and the touch of his skin against mine. Let's be honest...I missed that chocolate man!

It had been at least seven months since we'd engaged in any sexual contact with each other, and normally that would've pushed me out the door faster than you could blink. But I was determined within myself that I wouldn't become frustrated. Even though he hadn't done anything but kissed me in that amount of time, I still was determined to see it through.

It was hard to go to bed every night and lie in the same bed and not do anything, or even be tempted to; but I had a feeling with the way he was holding me in his arms that things were on the upswing of change. The way I felt at this moment made me feel like I was on top of the world and could conquer anything. Now, all I hoped was this feeling of euphoria was translated into our bedroom and that it happened soon, because even though I was developing the patience of Job, I didn't know when that stored up patience would choose to run out.

Chapter 2 (Randy)

How time brings about a change...
I'm looking in the face of the woman who I gave my last name to and I remember a time when this same woman could do no wrong in my eyes. I used to think Denise walked on water, but with time... comes change; and the true reality of it all is sometimes a hard pill to swallow.

I must admit it, I'm the guilty one that put my wife on a pedestal as if she carried a perfect existence. I raise my hand and take the blame for that, but I will not apologize for being head over hills in love. I love that woman with all my heart, soul, and mind, and maybe I became blind to our reality due to the magnitude of love I had for her. Who knows? All I know is I thought we had a solid marriage, but it couldn't be any more solid than a jar of baby food. Granted, we had counseled a few dozen couples, and conducted numerous pre-marital counseling sessions, but that didn't amount to a hill of beans when compared to the fact that our own marriage was on shaky ground.

Here I am the pastor of one of the largest congregations in the city of Youngstown, and married to one of the most beautiful women I've ever laid eyes on, and she's having a full-fledged affair behind my back. The icing on the entire situation was when I found out it was Tyrone. Before I found out his true reason for wanting to be a member of my church, I considered him to be one of the most dedicated men to ever step foot in my ministry.

I had always prided myself as a man who was able to have a healthy balance between ministry and family. Never in a million years did I think our marriage would be the very thing in limbo.

"Randy, did you hear what I just asked you?" Deacon Russell asked as he walked on the treadmill beside me. For a second I wanted to shake my head *yes* and pretended I knew what he had just asked me, but let's face it: my mind and my thoughts had drifted once again to another place and I didn't have a clue.

"No, Russ. I'm sorry; I didn't hear what you were saying." I answered and put my *iPod* on pause.

"Oh. I was just asking you if you thought the *Pittsburgh Steelers* were gonna have a good season this year but that's not important, it seems like you have a lot on your mind. What's up man?" Russell asked.

"A lot—too much man." I replied. I hoped that made enough sense to him, but knowing my good friend he was going to ask me to clarify and expound on my vague response.

"Come on Randy, talk to me. That's why I'm here. You can tell me what's troubling you."

If it's one thing I'm sure of, I know I can talk to Russell. He was not just one of my deacons from the church, but he had also grown to be a very good friend over the years. No matter what I was going through, I could always talk to him and he would listen. He wouldn't judge me at all. He and Sheila had given me some of the best marital advice this side of heaven. Their wisdom was unmatched to anyone else I knew well; besides my parents that is. No offense to my mother and father, but sometimes I needed advice from someone who was on the outside looking in.

"Well, as you know, Denise and I are really trying to work on our marriage and get through this situation but we are still having some problems." I explained, trying not to go into full detail. I knew I could still talk to Russell, but I wasn't sure if I wanted to disclose this type of information to him.

Jessica A. Robinson

"Okay, what kind of problems?" Russell asked. I paused for a moment, wrapped my earphone wires around my *iPod* and then cleared my throat.

"I mean we're just having problems in other areas Russ..." I looked at him and gave him a certain look that he immediately caught on to. I'm so glad he got the hint because we were in the middle of the gym and for it to be early in the morning; the gym was kind of crowded.

"Oh, you mean ya'll are having sex problems?" he asked.

I nodded.

"Has your sex life completely changed?"

"Dramatically." I answered.

"Meaning?"

"Meaning we don't have sex at all anymore. We haven't been intimate since before Kaylah was born and for us, that's bad. We had a very healthy sex life before all this happened." Russell scratched his head for a second as if he was in deep thought.

"Hmmm...so have you two tried to do anything at all?"

"She's tried numerous times, and I always hit her with an excuse like; I'm tired, I don't feel like it, or I fall asleep in my office to avoid turning her down all together."

"Wow, so is your hesitation coming because of the affair?" Russell asked, as I stopped walking on my treadmill altogether.

"Yeah, I've sat and thought about everything for months and that's honestly where my hesitation stems from."

"Do you still love Denise?"

"Of course I love her, and I'm still *in love* with her too, but I still have a lot of things to work through when it comes to the sex thing."

"That's understandable. When Denise cheated on you she violated your trust, and once trust is gone, it

HOLY REVENGE

takes a while to get it back. It's a common thing that couples go through when infidelity is involved."

"I guess I just never thought Denise and I would be having intimacy problems because we've never had them in the past."

"Well, Randy, it happens to the best of us, and I'm just glad Sheila and I lasted as long as we have in order to be able to encourage you and Denise today."

"Sheila cheated on you Russ?" I asked.

"No, I cheated on her. It was a long time ago, and although I'm not proud that I stepped out on my wife, it still happened and I'll admit it—we separated for a period of time, but it all worked out and we made it through."

I was shocked to hear that Russell had been unfaithful to his wife in the past, but I guess the saying, "there's nothing new under the sun" is true. I could never picture him doing anything like that but then again I couldn't picture Denise doing anything like that either and she still did anyway.

"Man, I remember a time when Sheila wouldn't even look at me, let alone let me touch her; it was hard, but eventually everything returned to normal between us."

"Did it take a long time?"

"I'm not even going to lie to you. It definitely took some time, but all was restored with the good Lord's help."

I shook my head in agreement because God had restored Russell and Sheila's marriage to the point where it appeared as though they never even had any problems at all. I really hoped me and Denise's relationship would return to a normal place soon. Do you know how hard it is to resist a woman that is as fine as my wife is? Being up in that King size bed, with all that booty, hips, and thighs, and yet still resist the urge to want to lay my hands on something—and I'm not talking about prayer. It's been tough.

Jessica A. Robinson

It's not like I haven't wanted to be intimate with her, it's just that somewhere between my desires and actually going through with it, I stop myself. Every time I even get close to wanting to do something with her, I get these images in my head of her and Tyrone. And not just any image either. I get visions of them having sex, of her calling his name, and even of them getting freaky up in *our* bed. These imaginations are so vivid, you would've thought that I've actually walked in on them doing something; but I thank God, I haven't. I don't even care to know any details because I think all it would do is make my visions of them that much worse, and I don't want that.

I stay in God's face constantly about these thoughts that pop up in my head and although they haven't completely gone away, they've decreased. Thank God.

Just thinking about another man being in places that were only previously occupied by me, is enough to drive me completely insane; but I'm doing the best I can to deal with it all. When I made the decision to stay with Denise and work on our marriage, I knew there was going to be work involved, but this is definitely a full-time job.

I know you may be quite surprised to hear a Pastor talk the way I do, but I believe in being a hundred percent honest. At the end of the day, we're just people too. Sometimes we tend to have this larger-than-life existence like we don't have any problems or issues, but that's far from the truth. A lot of times we have the same amount of problems, if not more, than our church members and I'm no different.

I leave the gym after working out with Russell and took the short drive down to the church. I loved getting my early morning workout in before I started my day. For some reason, it seems to always set everything I have to do for the day in order, and order was something that I desperately need right now.

HOLY REVENGE

With Minister Willis resigning, and my secretary Tanisha having to leave for med school, I didn't know whether I was coming or going. Even though Willis was one of the many ministers that I had on staff at this point, he still helped to play an integral part in the ministry. Not only did he take it upon himself to start the single's ministry, but he also ran it and has done a fantastic job with maintaining it too.

He had developed and organized all kinds of events and programs that attracted singles from all over the tri-state area. No matter who you were, or what church you went to, you had heard about the events our singles were doing and I was proud of that fact. So when Willis announced he was leaving out of the blue, that completely threw me for a loop. I remember him saying something about how he had been praying and God told him his season at Oakdale was over and it was time for him to move on and do what God was calling him to do, but I didn't totally believe him. I mean, who am I to doubt that he is truly hearing from God, but something about his explanation sounded a bit rehearsed. Like he'd somehow fabricated the entire story and slapped God up in the mix so I wouldn't question his abrupt departure from the ministry, but whatever his reason is for leaving, I pray he truly hears from God and is in His will.

As far as Tanisha leaving, I knew it was going to happen. It was only a matter of time. When I hired her, I already knew she would be leaving once she got into medical school. There was no surprise there, but somehow I hoped it would take her a little longer to get into school; only because she's been such a wonderful secretary to me. Since she's been here, she's kept me so organized that I've been ahead of my schedule. It's been running so smoothly that my day ends at five in the evening every day. I'm really going to miss her.

My office phone rang and interrupted my thoughts. I glanced at my watch and then down at the caller ID and wasn't surprised to see my mother's number flashing across the screen. It never fails; my mother calls me at the same time every day.

"Hey mom, how are you?" I said, as I pressed the speaker button so I could continue to type on my sermon notes.

"I'm just fine son. I'm just calling to check up on you, what you up to?"

"I'm just doing a little work on this week's sermon. What are you and dad doing?" I asked.

"Well, I'm finishing up dinner and I just finished making two pans of banana pudding. Your father is in the den watching *ESPN*. Are you and Denise still coming for dinner tonight?"

Ahh, man, I totally forgot about that...

"Yes, ma'am. You know we'll be there. What time do you want us to come?"

"How about six?"

"We'll be there ma."

"Okay, well, I'll see ya then. Love you."

"Love you too." I hung up the phone and immediately dialed my wife's cell phone number.

I was so relieved when she picked up on the first ring.

"Hey baby, what are you doing?"

"Nothing right now. I'll be going out with Terri. We're going to the mall to get some things for Kaylah."

"What else does the baby need? She has more things than both of us combined." I laughed.

"I know it seems that way to you, but baby girl is growing out of all of her clothes and her godmother has been itching to buy her something, so we're going to the mall in a little while."

"Please don't be mad at me, but I forgot that Mom wants us to come over for dinner today. After you're done shopping can you meet me over there?"

"Yeah babe, that's no problem, that's actually great because I really didn't feel like cooking today."

"So I'll be going over there after five and we'll wait for you and Kaylah don't worry."

HOLY REVENGE

"Okay honey, well, I'm about to get me and the baby ready to go out. I'll see you in a little while."

"Okay Denise. I love you."

"Love you too, bye." I smiled as I hung up the phone. We may be having little issues within our marriage, but I loved that woman more than life itself. Since I consider myself to be a great man of faith, I believed our marriage would return back to the way things were, and I wouldn't be satisfied until they did. We may have our ups and downs, but most marriages did. Her affair was a hard thing for me to deal with every day, but when I took the vows standing at the altar the day she became my wife, I said, "for better or for worse" and I truly meant every single word.

My office phone rang again interrupting my thoughts and when I picked up the phone to say, 'hello', I couldn't even get that out real good before the person hung up. I stared at the phone for a few seconds before I placed it on the receiver. That was strange because I never really had anyone call me at the church and hang up on me unless it was like a telemarketer or someone selling something I didn't want. I wasn't alarmed too much at first, but I sure hoped that the person who loved to play on my wife's phone, wasn't taking the opportunity to start playing on mine.

By the time five o'clock came around, my sermon was done and printed up. I called everyone that I needed to call who were on my task list for the day. And I had even gone as far as doing a few other things that would need to be done in the morning, so I already had a jumpstart on everything and I was happy about that. I gathered my briefcase and my leather folder and locked up my office.

Walking down the hall, I saw Kenny sitting in his usual spot as his desk working on some paperwork.

"Hey Brother Kenny, I'm on my way out of here. I'll see you tomorrow; have a good evening."

"I sure will Pastor. I'll be leaving soon. As soon as I finish this paperwork up, I'm gonna make sure the building is secure and then I'll be on my way too."

"Okay, sounds good...thanks again for all your hard work. I know I always tell you this, but I really appreciate you and everything you do."

Kenny smiled.

"No problem Pastor. I take my job as the security guard for the church very seriously."

"Have a great evening."

One thing is for sure, Kenny surely did take his job as the security guard of my church seriously, and sometimes too seriously if you ask me; but to each his own. The way Kenny guarded our church you would think he was guarding the gold at Fort Knox. Ever since we hired him, he's watched over this place like a watchdog and I'm thankful for his dedication, although, he strikes me as a little odd at times. I guess you can say I'm more thankful than I am disturbed. I feel like security is a job and someone has to do it, so if it has to be Kenny, then I'm not the one to complain.

I pulled up to my mother's house and parked at the end of the driveway since there was an unfamiliar car parked behind my parent's Buick. My mother and father always had their friend's over on any given day for coffee and cake or just to sit around and catch up on conversation, so I figured it was one of their friends who had parked their Blue Jaguar XF behind their car. Before I made my way to the front door, I checked out the car; it was beautiful. I didn't know who the owner of this car was, but whoever it was they surely had it going on. I walked up to the front door and hit the doorbell. My mother came and opened the door immediately.

"Hey son. How are you? Where's Denise? Is she on her way in with the baby?" she asked as she looked past me to see if Denise was behind me. She was looking and acting nervous and I didn't have the slightest clue as to why.

HOLY REVENGE

"No ma. She's out with Terri at the moment, but she'll be on her way soon. Why? What's wrong?"

My mother looked behind her and then back at me.

"Nothing is wrong. Why did you say that son?" she asked. I stood back for a second and took in my mother's demeanor and overall attitude, and she definitely was nervous about something. I couldn't figure out what had my mom all antsy, but there definitely was something that had her all anxious and jumpy.

"I asked that because you're acting really jumpy and nervous mom. What's going on that has you like this?" I walked past her, shut the door behind me and continued on down the hallway into the family room where a woman stood looking on top of the fireplace on the mantle at all the pictures my parents had put up there. I knew only one person who looked the way she did, and I couldn't believe what my eyes was seeing. Even from behind I knew exactly who the woman was and when she turned around it was confirmed.

"Alexis?" I asked. Even though I knew it was Alexis, I felt like my eyes were somehow failing me. There was no way my childhood sweetheart, Alexis Wilson, was standing in my parent's house.

She smiled, revealing her dimples that I remembered her having as a child.

"Randy?"

"I'm sorry son, I didn't get a chance to tell you when you walked in that Alexis was here, but I'll leave you two alone, I must check on dinner." She said as she hurried out of the room and disappeared into the kitchen. That's why my mother was nervous. She usually was the epitome of composure and elegance, but Alexis Wilson had temporarily taken all of that away. And to make matters worse, she left me in that room, all alone, with the only other woman I've ever loved besides my wife.

Jessica A. Robinson

"Wow. You're the last person I ever expected to see here today." I said, as I walked over and gave her a quick hug. A quick hug was all I could give Alexis right now. I was trying to keep it as short and sweet as I could.

"I know you're surprised." she smiled.

"Am I? I almost had a heart attack when I saw you here just now" I laughed. "When's the last time you even came home to this area?"

"It's been almost fifteen years, and I felt like it was time I return home and see how much everything and everyone has changed."

"Fifteen years? That's a long time. Yeah, everything has definitely changed. How are your parents doing?" I asked as I sat down on the couch and she sat in the chair across from me.

"They're doing okay. You know my father is in a nursing home right now across town, and my mother still lives in the house I grew up in, but she is looking to sell her house so she can get a smaller place and move closer to him after he's done with rehabilitation."

"Yeah, my mother was telling me about your dad having hip surgery."

"He had it about six months ago and he's progressing fine. He should be back on his feet completely in the next month or so."

"Sounds good. I think I saw your mother outside two weeks ago watering plants and she still looks the same."

"Yeah. she does. I have to spend a lot of hours in the gym working out and eating right to keep up with her."

"So I take it that brand new car outside is yours huh?"

She shook her car keys in front of her.

"Sure is. I brought it like a month ago. Still have my temporary tags on it."

"That's a great car. You must be a rich woman buying cars like that."

HOLY REVENGE

Alexis tilted her head to the side slightly and smiled. Her doing that reminded me of all the times we used to talk when we were younger. She always made that gesture when she was in conversation with me.

"I wouldn't say I'm rich, but I work hard for the things I have. Being a dentist is hard work."

"Wow. You're a dentist. I never knew. After you left your senior year, it was like you vanished off the face of the earth. I didn't know where you were."

"I can see how you felt I disappeared, but I didn't. I was around." She smiled at me and although I smiled back, my mind took me back to fifteen years ago. It was funny to me how someone so beautiful could still be in so much denial after all these years. Alexis Wilson was the one woman, before Denise, that I loved.

She was my next door neighbor who I had grown up with my entire life, and we were in love with each other. From the time we could walk and talk, we had become best friends and we did everything together. I actually thought we would be married one day but shortly after she became a senior her feelings changed toward me.

I was a junior in high school, and even though I was younger than she was, I was confident in how I felt about her and my intentions toward her. At first I attributed it to her being a senior and all the things she had to do to get ready for college; but by the time she walked across the stage to get her diploma, she had told me she was accepting a scholarship to *Spelman College* and didn't think twice about me or our relationship.

Little did she know, but the summer before I had saved my entire summer job money and went and brought her an engagement ring. I had come to her graduation not only to support her, but also to propose to her, but when she walked off that stage and announced to me that she was moving to Atlanta in less than two weeks, there was nothing that I could say. I never mentioned anything to her. Up until this point, the last time I saw her was the day of her graduation party.

I was completely crushed, and have tried for the life of me to erase her memory, and all that she meant to me, out of my heart and my mind, but seeing her has made me feel something like I did for her all those years ago. Time and space will do that to you. It will remind you of some things in your past that you haven't let go of; and although I thought fifteen years had completely eradicated Alexis Wilson from my memory, she was still there front and center.

"No, you haven't been around. After graduation you left Youngstown and didn't look back. Now tell me if I'm lying."

"You make it seem like I turned my back on everyone that was here and left for school. I went to Atlanta to further my education, not to forget where I come from."

"Well, it surely seem like you forgot everything and everyone who meant anything to you. I thought I'd never see you again." I said as I looked over at Alexis trying to maintain my cool. I didn't want to appear as if I was upset after all these years, but I was. I was furious at how the one person I loved so much, could just up and leave without any regards to how I felt and what our relationship meant. I used to think she was going to be my wife, the mother of my children and we would live happily ever after, but I was so wrong.

"Junior, I never thought after all these years you would still be mad at me."

Junior. She was the only person who called me that when she was really trying to say something to me.

Hearing her call me by my childhood nickname felt more like an insult instead of a term of endearment. "Alexis please, let's not play these games. It's good to see you after all this time, but let's not act like we're old friends. We have a lot of issues to resolve and talk about before we get back to that point." I reminded her.

Instead of arguing the statement she made to me, she shook her head in agreement.

"You're right Randy. You're exactly right."

"So how long are you here for?"

"I'll be here for a few weeks. I would love to exchange numbers and maybe we can meet up while I'm here and talk about everything."

I handed her my phone and allowed her to punch her number in and then I saved it.

"How could I say no? You always had a way of persuading me to do anything. You forever had me in trouble when we were little." I started to laugh when I thought about the many times we had gotten into trouble together.

"I know you're not trying to blame all of the trouble on me, you were just as guilty as I was Randy!" She pointed her finger at me, twisted up her mouth and nose at me like she used to do and it sent us both into laughter.

"What's so funny?" Denise asked as she walked into the room and saw me and Alexis engaged in laughter and at that point I didn't see anything funny at all either. All I knew was tonight was going to be one of the longest dinners I ever had in my life.

Chapter 3 (Terri)

I don't claim to be an expert at many things, but there are a few areas in which I do excel. Being a lawyer is an area in which I feel I'm at the top of my game. I absolutely love what I do. I know law and legal procedures like the back of my hand, and I love practicing law so much that I would still do it even if I wasn't getting paid—well, let me rethink that, yeah, I still would be a lawyer without any monetary compensation on site.

I also feel that I'm an excellent daughter, friend, and Godmother. I love Kaylah as if she was my own daughter. Those are the other three areas I also feel I'm at the top of my game as well, but when it comes to this thing called, "Love", I don't even have a clue! This is all so new to me...

I've always been an independent woman, making my own money and supporting myself. I've dated around and hit the 'so called' dating scene with no success at all, and I decided to bow out gracefully and stopped dating altogether. I've dated men from all different walks of life. Rich ones, poor ones, successful ones, not so successful, work-a-holics, men whose idea of work is playing *X-box* all day, momma's boys, and men who had more felonies than hairs on their head. You name it, I've dated them. My self-imposed break from the dating game, I felt, was a smart move because I'd rather be happy and alone, than dating someone and be miserable.

Now I know you hear a lot of bitter women say they can do bad all by themselves, but I'm not coming from a bitter place. I truly meant what I was saying. I was way too focused to lose everything I had worked so hard for all because I was tied up with some no good man. I was focused and so content in my happy, little, single world, until one day when my business lunch at *Rosetta Stone* changed my entire world.

I was sitting at lunch with one of my fellow colleagues, Winston Christopher, and he was telling me some funny story about one of his children. His stories are hilarious and usually he pulls me right in because his children are absolutely crazy, but for some reason I found it hard to concentrate on what he was saying. Maybe it was due to the fact that I had a lot on my mind, or the fact that *Rosetta Stone* was unusually crowded for this time of day. Since my office was not too far from *Rosetta Stone*, I was afforded with the luxury of dining there more often than most people. And for some reason there were more people coming in and out than I had ever seen before.

Even though I had been listening to every word Winston was saying, I couldn't help but watch everyone that walked in the restaurant. Most were familiar to me. I recognized quite a few from working at various places downtown. Then out of nowhere, this fine man walks in and catches me completely off guard. I had seen many attractive men but none of them compared to the man right before my eyes. He appeared to be African-American, but something about his facial features and the texture of his hair, suggested he had Spanish ancestry. His black, curly hair, deep set dimples, and deep caramel colored skin, all let me know that he was probably mixed with Puerto Rican. The man was gorgeous!

I tried not to stare too hard at him, but it was something about the way he dressed, and the way he carried himself that commanded my complete attention. I could hear Winston was still engrossed in telling me his story, but I still can't even tell you a word he said. I occasionally nodded and threw in my two cents to give him assurance that I was listening, but I wasn't. My gaze and my attention were focused on two tables in front of me where this fine man sat with two other men. From first glance, it looked like they were in the middle of a meeting, although I wasn't really sure being so far away. I didn't care what they were talking about; all I wanted to do was watch this perfect specimen of a man. Just when I thought I was looking at him on the sly, he turned his head and looked directly at me.

Oh, shoot...

I had tried to turn my focus back on Winston and the one sided conversation that was going on at my table, but it was already too late. Mr. Fine Man had caught me red-handed. He looked over at me again and smiled teasing me with those dimples of his. Through his smile I also got a chance to see his beautiful set of white teeth. I smiled at him, took a deep breath, exhaled, and then turned back towards Winston who had just answered his ringing phone.

Before I could ask him who it was, he had excused himself from the table and walked out of the restaurant. I looked out of the corner of my eye at Mr. Fine Man and he just so happened to be at his table all alone. He looked over at me and smiled again. I couldn't help but smile back at this beautiful man. He didn't stop there. He got up from his table and walked over to mine. My heart began to pound heavily as he made his way over to where I was and asked,

"Do you mind if I sit down for a second?"

"No, I don't mind."

"Now, I normally don't approach total strangers like this, but your smile is so inviting I couldn't help myself."

"Thank you. You have a nice smile as well." I answered.

So not only was this man gorgeous, but he was charming too...I liked him already!

"My name is Carlos. Carlos Sanchez," he stuck out his hand and took mine in his.

"My name is Terri Jones."

HOLY REVENGE

"Such a beautiful name to go along with a beautiful person."

"Thank you again." I smiled and nodded.

"If I'm making you uncomfortable I'll stop. Don't want to make your lunch companion jealous."

What a clever way to ask me if I was taken...

"If that was your way of asking me if I was single or not, then the answer is, 'yes'. Actually my lunch companion is a lawyer at the firm I work at."

"Oh, so you're a lawyer?"

"Yes, that would be correct." I smiled. I swear I've never smiled this much in my life.

"So, you're beautiful *and* intelligent."

"Thanks again." He was really making me blush. This guy was too smooth. He probably was a player or something.

"And what is it that you do?" I asked.

"Oh, I work for an architectural firm from Texas, I'm an architect,"

I pressed my lips together, smiled, and shook my head up and down.

"Wow, an architect huh? That sounds like an interesting job." I leaned forward resting my elbows on the table. If he was any good at reading body language he would know that I was totally captivated and tuned into what he had to say.

"Yeah, I love what I do. I hope I'm not too forward but I would love to exchange numbers with you. Maybe we could go out sometime." Carlos suggested.

Usually when I meet men I don't give out my personal number. In this day and age you just never know who you're coming into contact with, but something about *him* suggested he was worth taking the risk. Before I could even control my actions, I took the phone he was holding in his hand, punched in my digits and handed it back to him.

"Call me." I winked.

Jessica A. Robinson

As he got up from the table, he smiled at me and said, "Don't worry, I will."

He definitely kept his promise and called me. Carlos and I have been inseparable ever since. Never thought I'd ever find someone I was truly compatible with until Carlos came along. I guess the saying, "Good things come to those who wait" is true because I've waited a long time to feel like this and I honestly wouldn't trade this feeling for the world.

****

"So Miss Lovey Dovey how are you and Mr. Sanchez doing?" Denise asked me as we sat across from each other at the Stonebridge Tavern. "We're fine. He's coming over to take me to dinner tonight." I smiled. I couldn't wait to see him later on. In my opinion, time wasn't moving fast enough.

"Aww that's so sweet...I wish I felt the same way about my husband at the present moment. I'm so mad at him right now." Denise crossed her arms and rolled her eyes.

"Why? What did Randy do?" I asked. I was surprised to even hear my best friend say she was mad at him because lately she had literally worshipped the ground he walked on. I know he's not perfect and can make mistakes like anybody can, but he had never really done anything to upset her.

"Girl, remember when we went shopping for Kaylah the other day and I told you we were having dinner at his parent's house?"

"Yeah, I remember," I closed my eyes and shook my head. "Please don't tell me you and Mama Tate are at it again."

"Nope, not at all."

I breathed a sigh of relief. Denise and her mother-in-law had just gotten back to a good place with each other and that's how they should stay. The way they were fighting with each other, you would've thought they were in the middle of World War II.

HOLY REVENGE

"So, after I left you, me and Kaylah went over to their house and when I pulled up I noticed a car I'd never seen before but I didn't think twice about it because Randy's parents are always entertaining their friends, but when I came in the house Randy was up in the living room laughing and talking with some woman!"

"What woman?—And why was she over your in-law's house in the first place?"

"Her name is Alexis and apparently, they were in a serious relationship right before we started dating."

"For real...that's funny because I've never heard you mention anything about someone by that name." I replied confused. I was pretty good with names and I didn't remember an *Alexis* ringing a bell.

"You're right. I never mentioned her because I didn't even know she existed until I met her that day." Denise stated as her nostrils began to flare. My mouth dropped. I could tell by the expression on her face that she was mad.

"So you mean to tell me you had no idea about this Alexis woman?"

Denise shook her head, *'no'*.

"I'm just as clueless as you."

"Wow. So what did Randy have to say for himself?"

"Sitting there all dumbfounded like he didn't know what to say. And then he gonna tell me that he didn't have a clue that she was coming over. And tried to feed me some crap like he hasn't seen her in years or something like that, but I don't believe that at all."

"Why don't you believe him?"

"Because for her to just be some old girlfriend he hasn't seen in a while, they were too comfortable with each other. Not to mention the way she was all flirty and giggly with my husband. I don't care what anyone says, she planned that visit."

Jessica A. Robinson

"That may be true, but I honestly don't think your husband would plan to meet up with some old girlfriend at his mother's house, especially since he knew you and the baby were on their way."

Denise held up her hands in surrender.

"Okay, I can see you're for team Randy." Denise cut her eyes at me.

Her little attitude didn't move me one bit. I wasn't afraid of her. I laughed at her remark.

"Whatever Denise. I'm not on anybody's side, but I think he may be telling the truth. Granted, I don't know why he's never told you about her, but that's just a subject that you two really need to discuss."

"Yeah, we're definitely going to have a talk about it all when I can stop being mad at him."

"Good." I answered.

"So enough about me. Carlos seems to be keeping a permanent smile on your face these days." Denise smiled from ear to ear and seeing her smile caused me to do the same.

Just hearing my sweetheart's name brought yet another smile to my face. I couldn't help but smile when I thought about him.

"Yeah, he kinda has that effect on me." I added.

"He must be a very special man if he got you acting like this."

"He's got skills...definitely." I winked.

"Eww...you're so nasty."

"Well, hey, I'm just keeping it real. He is a very special man indeed."

"I hear you. I'm just glad you're happy. You deserve to be happy and I'm glad that Carlos can do that for you."

"Yes, and he does a wonderful job of that."

"Well, just promise me you won't run off and elope."

"I'll never do that. You know my mother will never let me live that down if I did something like that.

HOLY REVENGE

Besides, when I get married, I want him to be the Pastor giving me my vows.”

“You already know that goes without saying.”

“I don’t want to speak prematurely Denise, but I think Carlos might end up being the one for me.”

“What do you mean the one?”

“You know what I mean. He might end up being my husband one day, but who knows? All I’m doing is taking things one day at a time.”

“And that’s all you can do. You’ll know if he is or not.”

After I got home from going to lunch, I decided to take a nap before I went out with Carlos later that evening. I didn’t really think I was tired until I stretched out across my plush, King-size bed. I allowed myself to drown into my comforter and pillows, and I was out before my eyes could close all the way. By the time I finally woke up, Carlos was actually nudging me.

“Baby wake up. We gotta get going if we’re going to make our dinner reservations on time.”

“Hey baby.” I yawned.

“How long have you been trying to wake me up?”

“Not long, but I’ve been blowing your cell phone up and when you didn’t answer I figured I’d use my key and come in because you were probably sleep and I guessed right.”

“That’s crazy, because I thought I was only going to lie down for a little while and that was three hours ago. I must’ve been tired.” I yawned again.

Carlos laughed.

“Babe tired is an understatement, you were exhausted. I told you all of those long hours you’re putting in at the firm was gonna catch up with you.”

“Whatever, I can handle it.” I answered.

Even though I didn’t want to admit it, Carlos was right. The hours I put in at the law firm were quite exhausting and although I’ve worked pretty much the same schedule since I first became a lawyer, I'm not as young as I used to be.

"You can be in denial if you want to, but you know I'm telling you the truth."

"I'm not in denial."

"Okay, Ms. Denial so can you get ready so we can go out to dinner please?" He leaned in and gave me a quick peck on my lips.

"I sure can. Give me twenty minutes." I said, springing out of bed as I walked straight into the bathroom. I'm glad I already set my clothes out before I fell asleep, so all I had to do was take a quick shower. Carlos was spread out on the couch in my bedroom flipping through channels on my flat screen T.V.

I heard his phone ring as I started the water running in my shower and then I heard him shut off my T.V. and walk out of my room and go back downstairs. That didn't really strike me as odd because he was always receiving business calls throughout the day. Once I got dressed, I came downstairs to find Carlos wasn't in sight. I could hear his voice and from the sound of it he was down the hallway in my office with the door closed. I walked down the hallway quietly, making sure I didn't make a sound. I walked up close to the door and put my ear to the door so I could listen in to his conversation. I couldn't figure out who he was talking to, but I could tell he was in deep conversation with whoever it was.

"Estella, I'm trying to figure out how you got this number. This is my personal line. You can call me at home if you have anything you need to say to me, but do me a favor and lose this number. I'm not trying to argue with you, just leave me alone for real. Goodbye."

I hurried away from the door and made my way to the kitchen. I didn't expect him to end his phone call so abruptly, and I didn't want him to think I was eavesdropping in on his conversation even though I was. I was relieved that I was able to take a seat at my kitchen table before he saw me.

HOLY REVENGE

"Hey babe. I'm ready to go." I smiled as I got up from the table and gave him a hug and a kiss.

"Okay, I'm ready too. I'll be waiting in the car." He replied and then walked out of the kitchen without warning. I could tell he was really upset about something. I had never seen him this way. Whoever had called him had put him in a bad mood and made him mad because he didn't say one word the entire drive to the restaurant.

At first I didn't press the issue, maybe he needed a few minutes to collect his thoughts and pull himself together. A few minutes turned into thirty and that eventually turned into an hour. After we received our dinner and he still hadn't said a word, I decided to address the silence.

"Why are you so quiet babe, what's wrong?" I asked.

He continued eating his salmon and rice pilaf for another moment and then he set his fork and knife down.

"I'm fine. Why you ask that?

Now, I definitely didn't want to say, *well, honey I was eavesdropping on your conversation and I know that some woman named Estella has made you mad.* So, I just kept it short and to the point.

"I don't know. You've been real quiet since we left my house and usually you're never this quiet. What's wrong?"

"Nothing to bother you with. Just a bill collector that called in and got up underneath my skin." I nodded at his explanation.

"That's all." He added and then grabbed my hand.

Now he must think I was born yesterday but that's definitely not the case at all. I don't care how many bill collectors call my house and cell phone harassing me, none of them have pissed me off to the point where my entire night is ruined, and I'm for sure not calling them by their first name like we're old friends. I have no clue who the heck Estella is, but trust and believe, I am going to find out sooner or later.

"Okay baby. If you ever want to talk about it I'm, here for you. I can even show you a few things to get the bill collectors to stop harassing you."

"Wow. Thanks babe! I really appreciate it." He said as he kissed my hand.

Yeah, it's okay Mr. Smooth Man you may not tell me who Estella is right now, but I was one of the best lawyers in the city and the state for that matter. The truth would come out sooner or later and when it was time to present my case I would remind him of this very moment.

HOLY REVENGE

Chapter 4 (Denise)

I sat next to Randy as he flipped through channels on cable. He pretended to tune me out as he watched his sports but I didn't care one bit, because I was doing the same thing as I looked through stacks of magazines I had received for the month.

It had been two whole days since we had spoken to each other, and with the way I was feeling I could go two more days without saying anything to him.

We took our turn stealing glances at each other while we thought the other wasn't looking, and I even added a few sighs and smacked my lips extra hard a few times to add to the dramatics of it all.

Yeah, I know me and husband look very childish right now to you but who isn't a little juvenile at times especially when you're mad? The point was, Randy had made me extremely mad the other day and I wanted him to know that I was still upset with him. After about thirty minutes of this foolishness Randy placed the T.V. on mute, set the remote on the coffee table, and then looked over at me. I saw him out of the corner of my eye but I acted like I didn't see him at all. I continued doing exactly what I had been doing.

"Denise." Randy called my name and I didn't even do so much as to flinch.

"Denise do you hear me?" he asked. I closed my magazine, placed it in my lap and then I answered him.

"Yes, I hear you."

"Oh, so you just weren't going to respond?"

"I'm responding now aren't I?" I asked in a sarcastic tone.

"So, I take it you're still mad about the other day?"

"And you're surprised?"

"I just don't see why you're so upset Denise. I had no way of knowing Alexis was going to show up at my parent's house unannounced. I haven't seen her in fifteen years."

"Yeah, whatever. You really expect me to believe you after you never even told me she existed? That wasn't right, and you know it."

Randy took a deep breath and then exhaled. He knew I had a point.

"I admit me not telling you about Alexis from the beginning was wrong, but I had my own reasons for doing so."

"And what reasons were those? You didn't want me to know about her because you still have feelings for her or something? You plan on trying to rekindle your relationship with her? What is it Randy? What is it, because people don't usually keep a person a secret for nothing." I explained.

"Come on baby. Don't be silly. I'm not interested in Alexis anymore. What she and I had was in the past, and I need for you to understand that."

"Oh, I understand alright. I understand you were trying to go around and be sneaky and this whole situation has backfired in your face."

"I'm being sneaky? I'm the one who's being sneaky? If anyone's sneaky, it's definitely you. I've never lied about who she was to me, and I would never do anything like that to you!"

"I never accused you of lying. I just wonder how Alexis has never come up in even one conversation we've had if she was such a huge part of your past."

"Because I didn't feel the need to say anything about her, that's why."

"Well, how about you say something about her now, because inquiring minds want to know."

"I've already explained who she was on the way home the other day." I put on the fakest smile I could muster up.

"Humor me and tell me again."

"Fine! Alexis has been my next door neighbor since before I can remember, and we were best friends all during school and growing up. We started dating seriously in high school, and broke things off when she went away to college. It's been fifteen years since I've seen or talked to her. I didn't know she was coming over and that's all. That's my story." Randy replied, and I rolled my eyes at him. I swear I felt like he was lying to me, but he told me the same exact story from the other day, and either he was telling the truth, or he had one hell of a memory. The only choice I had was to believe him at this point.

"So, you're telling me that you haven't had any previous contact with her until then?"

"Not at all. I know it's hard for you to believe me, but in the entire time we've been married I've never lied to you. I know you have a problem with lying; but I don't. I've been completely honest with you and I plan on staying that way. She was a part of my past that I didn't want to bring up because there was some hurt involved in our relationship, and that's why I never said anything to you about her. Now I would appreciate it if we could drop this whole subject...please." He stated as he got up from the couch. He walked away from me and started in the direction of the stairs.

"Where are you going?" I asked as I saw him walking up the steps.

"Jimmy and I are going golfing. If you want to, I can have him call you, check in and verify that it's just me and him on the course since you obviously think I'm being sneaky." Randy said as he kept on walking into our bedroom and slammed the door shut.

Well, I can't say I didn't deserve that remark Randy made, because I did. I don't know why I couldn't just trust him at his word and what he was telling me, or even why I felt the need to make my own assumptions about the whole situation. It was just something that I did. Randy is right though. He has never given me a reason to think otherwise. He's always been up front and honest with me about everything. If there was anyone to question in our relationship, it would be me. If you compare me to my husband, I should be the one being interrogated like I was on an episode of *Law and Order*.

I felt stupid for coming at him like that, but it was too late now, and I couldn't take any of it back. All I could do was try my best and make up for it. Once Randy left the house, I left the baby with Marisol and I decided to go to the store and pick up a few things that were sure to reiterate my sincerest apology.

After our little dispute, I decided I was going to cook him his favorite meal. When he walked through the door that evening, I already had Kaylah in bed, and I was waiting on him with a black lace negligee I purchased from *Macy's* last week. Even though everything within me wanted to ask him where in the hell he had been since I know golf doesn't last twelve hours, I resisted the urge to do so. I was in the frame of mind of making up to my husband, and I would've been a complete fool to waste an entire evening that took me the whole day just to set up. I was trying to apologize and make love to him too. I knew if he wasn't going to initiate sex, then at least I could take the first step and make something happen, but I was wrong about that one. Randy wasn't in the mood at all, and fed me yet another excuse. At that point, I don't even remember what his excuse was because I was too pissed off to listen to anything else. Here I had spent an entire day trying to let him know that I was wrong, and once again I had put my foot in my mouth, and all I wanted to do was to end the evening the way a husband and wife should, and that was having sex...yet he denied me once again.

Jessica A. Robinson

I let out another yawn, and then looked at my alarm clock that sat next to me on the nightstand. The alarm had buzzed and it was time for me to get up and start my day and I had so many things planned that I had to do; I had no choice but to get up early.

"Good morning baby. How did you sleep last night?" Randy yawned as he got up from his side of the bed and stretched. His yawning was contagious and I found myself doing the very same thing before I answered him.

"I slept okay. Did you get some shut eye?" I asked.

"Yeah, I slept like a baby." He smiled at me and then kissed my forehead. For all I cared, he could've kept his little kisses.

"Thank you for last night. I enjoyed everything." He replied.

Well, I enjoyed everything up until he didn't want to give me what I wanted. That's when the night turned bad for me and because I was trying my best not to argue, I just let it all go.

I know I had lied about getting some good rest, but I wasn't in the mood to be upset and I definitely wasn't in the mood to argue about why I wasn't able to get a wink of sleep. There was an ounce of me that did want to tell him the truth, but I wasn't so sure I wanted to go *there* with him. What I really felt like telling him is I spent my entire night staring at the wall trying to figure out why he was never in the mood to have sex with me anymore. I had a meeting at the church with the women's committee which wasn't for another two hours, and all I wanted to do was sleep just a little longer but when I heard Kaylah making noise from her room, I knew it was time to get up.

"Babe, where you going?" Randy asked as he saw me put on my pink silk robe and slippers.

"To get the baby, I can hear her."

"Oh, okay. Come back so we can all lie around for just a little while until we have to leave. I love just

HOLY REVENGE

being able to be near you and hold you." Randy smiled as I tied up my robe.

"I love you too." I answered and walked out of the master bedroom down the hallway.

There's something else that I love to do, but the reality is we don't do it at all anymore. And that's the gospel truth.

I walked into Kaylah's room and saw her sitting up in her crib smiling from ear to ear and all I could do was smile. It didn't matter how frustrated or mad I was about something, just one look at my little girl erased away all the negativity I was experiencing. I picked her up out of the crib and discovered her diaper was wet so I walked over to the changing table and put her on a new diaper. When we made it back to the master suite, Randy told me he was going to take a quick shower which left me and the baby alone in the huge King-sized bed. I picked up the remote and turned on the forty-two inch plasma screen that was mounted on the wall.

Before I could even flip through any channels my *Blackberry* began to vibrate. I picked it up and saw the familiar unknown number flashing across the screen. Against my better judgment, I decided to answer it.

"Hello." I pushed the talk button and then pressed the phone up to my ear.

"Denise, I'm so glad you answered your phone. I've been trying to reach you for some time." I paused before answering and then continued.

"Darnell? What are you doing calling me from this number?"

"I recently got my number changed."

"But I thought you were moving to North Carolina?" I asked and then glanced at the bathroom where Randy was still taking a shower because I could hear the water running and him humming a melody to a song.

"Oh, those plans fell through, besides I was offered the opportunity to become director here at the gym and you know I couldn't pass that position up."

"Cool."

"I apologize for calling you from an unknown number, but I had no other way of getting in touch with you."

"Well, what's up?" I asked curious to find out why he was so adamant about reaching out to me.

"I was hoping that we were still cool enough where we could meet up. I really would like to talk to you about some things."

Just as I was getting ready to answer him I heard Randy stepping out of the shower.

"Look we're still cool and all, but I don't think it's a good idea to be meeting up anywhere. I gotta go. Bye." I hung up without even giving him a chance to respond.

That was one person I never expected to hear from again. I had brief words with him at the funeral and when he contacted me a week later trying to strike up conversation, I told him for the sake of my marriage that it was better that we had no contact with each other.

Truthfully, Darnell had never done anything to me that caused me to feel the way I do, but I considered him to be guilty by association. And if Randy had found out that I was keeping in touch with one of Tyrone's blood relatives, it would cause even more trouble in our marriage. I scrolled down to Darnell's number and saved it into my contacts as *Danielle,* and I did so just in the nick of time.

"Hey babe, who were you on the phone with?" Randy asked as he came over and sat down on the bed picking Kaylah up.

"Oh, that was Sister Daphne. She was just making sure our meeting was still on." I answered.

Randy looked at me and then smiled. "Good 'ol Daphne. That woman don't miss a beat."

HOLY REVENGE

I laughed.

"She sure doesn't."

We all lay around in bed for a little while and then after the baby fell asleep I decided to get up and get dressed. I kissed Kaylah on her cheek and Randy got up from bed to hold me in his arms. It felt so good being embraced by him and even though we weren't having sex at the moment just his touch felt like heaven.

I pulled up in the parking lot of *The Mocha House* and noticed Daphne waiting for me in her silver Buick Regal. I giggled as I thought about the comment my husband made before I left the house. Daphne had to be the nosiest woman in the entire congregation. She was the type of woman who you didn't want to tell your business to, because she couldn't keep anything to herself. The woman couldn't hold water and everyone knew it. She always had to *run and tell* what she knew to anyone who would listen, and the fact that she was a busybody drove me crazy, but she was undeniably one of the most dedicated women in the church. So when I formed the committee for the women's conference, I knew I needed to include Daphne on my team. Of course the inclusion came with a price, but I agreed to grin and bear it. At least for now anyway.

"Good Morning Sister Daphne." I said, as I got out of the car and pressed the red button on my key ring for the alarm. Daphne quickly rolled her eyes and then smiled.

"Good Morning First Lady. For a second there, I thought you weren't coming. You know punctuality is a good characteristic that every first lady should possess."

"It sure is, and we're still waiting on a few women to arrive; so we'll be fine. I'm right on time." I chose to smile. completely ignoring her smart comment. It was too early in the morning and too beautiful of a day to be dealing with her controlling and

Jessica A. Robinson

opinionated behind. The only way I was going to be able to get through this meeting was to ignore her.

"If you say so."

Daphne emerged from the car apparently dressed in her Sunday best, and looked nothing less than casket sharp. I looked her up and down, checking out her appearance. Daphne was dressed in a navy blue church suit with the skirt that fell almost to the floor. She had on two-inch navy heels with thick stockings that made her skin appear like it was pasty. Daphne had the nerve to top off her entire look with a pair of white gloves. You know the kind that deaconess wear in church for communion. I did everything within my power not to burst out laughing as I visually took in her ensemble.

"I see you're all dressed up. Do you have somewhere else to be after our meeting?" I asked as we walked across the parking lot toward the entrance of the coffee house.

"No, why did you ask me that? Do you have somewhere else to be?" Daphne repeated what I said, only adding to my irritation. I absolutely hated when Daphne felt the need to repeat what I asked her. She must've known it got on my nerves because she always did it; as if to annoy me.

"No, I was asking you because I see you're all dressed up. I was just wondering."

"Well, just because you choose to come out of your house dressed like you're going to a party, doesn't mean I have to do the same. I take great pride in how I present myself, but I can't say that everyone else does the same." Daphne fired back and shot me a look. I didn't know what she was hinting at, especially when I was hardly underdressed. I didn't think skinny jeans, high heels, and a ruffle dress shirt was how you would go to the club, but Daphne apparently was going to have her own opinion—regardless.

HOLY REVENGE

"And where is everyone else at? What time did you tell the other women to meet us here?" Daphne glanced down at her watch.

"Relax. I spoke with my mother-in-law and the other two ladies, and they're all within five minutes from being here."

We walked in and found a comfortable spot that was tucked away in a corner. When we sat down, my mother-in-law walked in.

"Hey ladies." She smiled and took her sunglasses off of her face and placed them in a case before stuffing it inside her brown leather *Dooney and Bourke* purse.

"Hey mom." I got up and gave her a big hug.

"Hey Denise, I'm sorry I'm late. Daddy Tate was late bringing me the car. He took it to get washed and waxed."

"It's not a problem at all; we actually just got here ourselves." I pulled out the seat next to me so she could sit down. Daphne cut her eyes at Alice, and as a result she took her good old time to respond. Five minutes had elapsed before she looked over at Daphne and acknowledged her presence.

"Daphne." Alice responded dryly.

"Alice." Daphne replied as she pressed her thin lips together in an attempt to suppress her attitude; which she didn't do a good job of at all. The waitress came by the table and took their orders. Daphne glanced down at her watch and then at the door.

"Are you sure Sister Carol and Tanisha are coming to this meeting? They're mighty tardy." Daphne commented.

"Oh, no need to get all worked up because here they both come now." Alice pointed in the direction of the door. I was relieved to have the entire committee in attendance so Daphne would leave me alone and shut her big mouth. I was getting tired of answering the same question over and over. Now we would be able to get started on the very reason we had come together in the first place. I had called a final meeting to finalize all the plans for our upcoming women's conference that was in one week.

"Okay ladies, let's get started right away. Mom, can you open us up in prayer?"

Alice nodded and signaled for the women to join hands. Everyone seemed to comply with her request except for the thorn in her side. Just as Alice was about to tell Daphne about herself, she joined hands with Tanisha and Carol and closed her eyes. Alice quickly rolled her eyes and then bowed her head in prayer.

"Precious Lord, we thank you for the opportunity to be gathered together again. We ask that you bless every woman here, as well as the women who will be attending our upcoming conference. Help us to have a productive meeting, in Jesus name, Amen."

The women said Amen in unison and took their seats. I didn't waste any time in taking control of the meeting.

"So, as you all know, we're about one week out from our women's conference and I called this meeting just to make sure everything is in line." I said, pulling a small blue notebook out of my purse.

"Carol, how is the food coming along? Is every meal in place for the entire conference?"

"Yes. I actually just spoke with the kitchen staff, and everything is completely squared away. The only thing they need from you is the menu for the private luncheon you and Pastor are having with all of the special guests."

I jotted down a note and then replied.

"Okay, I'll have that for them by tomorrow."

"So, Tanisha what are our registration numbers looking like?" I asked.

The young, twenty-something woman with multi-layered, shoulder length hair smiled before she spoke.

HOLY REVENGE

"Well, as of this morning, we have fifteen hundred women registered for the event, but that number will only continue to grow during the first day of the event." When I heard those numbers escape from her lips all I could do was smile.

"That's wonderful. Do we still have commercials running on *JAMZ 101.9*?"

"Yes, but since it's the last week they will air it, we've paid for additional time so they can be played on *T-LUV's* show in the afternoon, and again on the evening show."

"That's a great idea." Alice remarked.

Daphne didn't allow their praises to resonate in the atmosphere very long before she interjected.

"Fifteen hundred? I would've expected our attendance to be well into the two thousand mark by now."

"Well, I'm not surprised; you know how church folks are. They operate in doing things at the last minute, and this conference won't be any different. Our numbers will jump considerably the first day, that's how it always is. Have no fear Daphne." Alice replied curtly, and pressed her lips together emphasizing her point.

"Okay, since everything else is taken care of, this brings us to our next item on our agenda; have you received final confirmations from all our speakers and our musical guests?" I turned my complete attention toward Daphne. Since she was always focusing on what everybody else was doing, or wasn't doing, I was eager to see if she had actually done her part.

"I'm pleased to announce that I received all of the email confirmations from our speakers for the event, as well as, our musical guest Xavier Latrell." Daphne said, as she slid a stack of paper toward me.

"Excellent." I replied and then let a smile sweep across my face. Not only was I excited that everything was starting to come together, but I was even more excited that we were able to lock in Xavier Latrell, who was one of the most popular praise and worship leaders in gospel music; not to mention, one of the finest men I had ever laid eyes upon. When we had begun the preliminary planning he had been one of the top people that the women of the congregation were requesting and I knew exactly why. With green eyes, deep set dimples, and caramel skin; his looks made him absolutely irresistible to all of his female supporters. He was very easy on the eyes and another plus was the fact that Xavier was a very single man and wasn't ashamed to admit it. I remembered seeing quite a few interviews where he boldly proclaimed that he was single, but in prayer for God to give him his wife. Since most women felt they had a chance to get his attention, this made him even more attractive to his female audience. And not only did he look delicious, he had the voice of an angel and wrote the type of songs that pierce the very bottom of your heart. Put it like this...Xavier Latrell had it going on. Having him on the roster for our upcoming event was the best decision we had ever made.

"Thank you Daphne, I'm so glad that everything is in place. Well, it seems like we're done with everything that I wanted to address. If you ladies don't have anything else then we'll close out in prayer." I said closing my notebook and sliding it inside my purse. I then glanced over at Daphne who snapped her fingers as if she'd forgotten to say something.

"Oh, before I forget, we have one special request from one of our speakers." She announced.

"And what is that?"

"Myra Washington, our speaker from Atlanta, will be arriving an entire day early and is requesting to be picked up by the first lady." Daphne looked over at me. I was completely confused.

"Did you explain to her that our transportation department would be there to get her once her flight comes in?"

HOLY REVENGE

"That's the thing. I explained all of that to her, but she still insisted on you coming,"

I just shrugged my shoulders. I didn't know what else to say.

"If she wants me to pick her up, I can. It's not a problem." I replied hoping that none of the women would pick up on the fact that I had a slight attitude. Out of all the requests I could've received, why did that request have to be made? Why wasn't our regular transportation good enough to pick Myra up? As if I wasn't already busy enough, now I had to add that to my laundry list of duties to do, but I was willing to be irritated and do what was asked of me if it meant that the event would be flawless. I figured if I could pull off the perfect conference that would grant me some extra points with my husband, then maybe he would take me off of punishment sooner rather than later.

Chapter 5 (Randy)

"**S**on, I really want to apologize for the other day. I had no idea Alexis was going to pop up over here." My mother said as I walked in the house behind her and shut the door behind me.

"Ma, it's okay. I know you had no idea that she would show up like that. It's been a very long time since she's been home; besides, I saw the look that was plastered all over your face when I discovered she was here."

If looks could kill, my mother would sure enough be six feet under. She was usually a woman with much composure and grace, but when she let me in the house the other day, I knew there was something wrong, I just didn't know what until I walked into the family room and discovered for myself.

"When she showed up at the front door unannounced, I really thought she would only stay for a few minutes, but then we got to talking about old times, her parents, and when she mentioned she was hungry, I told her she could stay without even thinking twice about it. It all just happened so fast. I'm sorry."

"You don't have to explain to me mom. I know you would feed the entire world if you could." Even though my mother was only cooking for a few people, she always prepared meals as though she was cooking for an army. People from the neighborhood, friends, and relatives always knew they could get a home-cooked meal if they stopped by, and usually our house was full with someone who couldn't get enough of my mother's southern cooking. She sure knew how to put her foot in a pot like nobody's business.

"Besides ma, the damage has already been done." I laughed.

"So, I take it Denise was mad huh?" My mother asked.

"Mad was definitely an understatement. She didn't talk to me for a few days behind this Alexis stuff. We're just getting back to being on good terms with each other."

"What was she mad about son?"

"She was upset because she had no clue who Alexis was, and when she walked in, we were laughing and in the middle of a conversation and she made her own assumptions from there."

"So, let me guess, she thinks you're cheating?"

"Yup."

My mother threw her hands up and laughed a little.

"You can't be serious."

"Ma, I wish I was lying to you right now."

"I can't believe her. So, that's why she went without speaking to you?"

"Yeah, because she felt like I was hiding something since I never told her about Alexis, and no matter what I told her, she just didn't feel like I was telling the truth. You know how hard it is to change a woman's mind once it's made up."

"You got that right. You ain't neva' lied about that one right there. Now, I'm not trying to be up in your business, but there are other things she should be focusing on rather than trying to accuse you of lying and being unfaithful. She has enough things on her plate other than trying to run behind you."

"I agree mom, but Denise will be Denise. Ever since she had that affair, she's been consumed with the fact that I'm going to cheat on her as some sort of revenge, but I would never do anything like that to her."

"Don't worry baby. Just keep being who you are, and doing what you're doing. Things will return to normal between you two trust and believe." My mother smiled and gave me a hug. She always knew exactly what to say to make me feel better. That's why I love talking with her.

"Thanks mom. I appreciate you."

"Well, I didn't want to keep you long, I just wanted to talk to you and make sure everything was okay since we have the women's conference coming up and all."

"Everything is fine. Tell dad I stopped by and I want some of the fish he catches this afternoon too." I said, as I walked over to the door and opened it slightly.

"I sure will son. Thanks for coming by."

"Oh, and before I forget, please tell Will I will be over here in a few days to whip him up in some basketball." My mother chuckled as she followed me to the door.

"I'll make sure I'll give him the message." She replied shutting the door and locking it.

I walked down the steps and was on my way to get in my truck and leave when I noticed Alexis' car was parked in her parent's driveway. I also noticed she had several pieces of luggage sitting out in the lawn, and it looked as though she was carrying it all into the house. I stood there for a moment until she came back out of the house breathing heavy and wiping her forehead which was covered in sweat.

She tried to jog down the porch steps, but ended up tripping on the last one.

"Do you need some help?" I asked, even though all I wanted to do was laugh. I didn't want to make her feel bad so I kept my laughter to myself.

"Um, I think I got it." She said, as she steadied her balance. Then she looked around and replied, "Well, maybe I do need a little help."

I tucked my keys in my pocket and walked across the yard and picked up a suitcase and a duffel bag. I followed suite right behind her into the house. I

HOLY REVENGE

moved as fast as I could and within fifteen minutes, I had successfully moved all of her things inside.

"Thank you so much. I really appreciate your help."

"It's no problem. I saw you needed an extra pair of arms, so I was glad I was able to help out. For you to only be here for a few days, you surely do have a lot of stuff."

"Oh, I'll be here a few weeks, so I brought more than I usually would."

"Okay, well, I guess I'll see you around." I replied walking to the door.

"Wait a minute. I have some chocolate chip cookies that just came out of the oven. Please stay and have a few. I even have some milk to go along with it." She smiled and walked off to the kitchen before I could protest. It wasn't like I was going to protest because I loved chocolate chip cookies. They were my absolute favorite. They were the one thing that Alexis mother, Brenda, would make every Sunday, and the heavenly scent from the oven would escape from their house and across the way into my bedroom and literally call my name until I couldn't resist anymore, and I found myself over their house posted up until they were coming out of the oven. It was no surprise that the memories of being over their house for hours all came back to me as I inhaled the same familiar scent. As she brought the plate of cookies and small pitcher of milk I was reminded of her mother doing the same thing and it caused me to smile.

"What you smiling at?"

"I was thinking about how your mom would conveniently make them for me every week."

"You're the only reason why she would make them so much. When I used to ask her to make them, she wouldn't move an inch."

"Wow. I never knew that."

"What? You were her little angel."

"I love your mom. How is she doing?"

Jessica A. Robinson

"She's doing good. Just settling into her new apartment and getting everything ready for my father when he comes home from the rehab center."

"Oh, that's good. It's hard to believe that they are selling this house after all these years."

"I know it was hard for me to believe they were, until I came home and saw for myself. I didn't want them to let go of the house, but it will be way easier for my father to get around while he heals, and having them in an apartment on one floor will be easier for them to manage right now."

"That makes perfect sense. I'm glad they're doing okay. Can you please tell them I asked about them?"

"Yeah, I will. They've asked me have I seen you."

Alexis offered me the plate full of cookies and I took a few off of the top. She poured me a glass of milk and I sat for a second and enjoyed the cookies. I couldn't even lie. Her cookies tasted just like her mother's and before I knew it I had already ate three cookies.

"Slow down. You're gonna eat the entire plate." She laughed.

"I'm sorry, but your cookies taste just like how your mom used to make them. She made a tin of cookies for Christmas last year and I have wanted some more ever since she made that batch for me."

"Well, I'm glad you like them. I wasn't going to make anything, but when I got in here and started remembering the old times, I just couldn't help myself." She smiled.

"I better get going. I have a lot of things to do today."

"Okay, well, I don't want to keep you, but you are more than welcome to stay for a while if you'd like."

I glanced down at my watch and forgot that I had somewhere that I needed to be.

HOLY REVENGE

"You know what, I have to get going. I have to meet my wife somewhere, but thanks for the invitation. Maybe next time." I said as I offered a polite smile and started walking.

"Of course, well, take care and I'm sure I'll see you around."

I walked back to my truck and could hear my phone ringing on the front seat. When I opened my door I could see my wife's number flashing across the screen. By the time I answered her call, she'd already hung up so I decided I would call her back when I got closer to home. I noticed that she had called me ten times, back to back, and I hoped that nothing was wrong, but I doubted it was because out of all those calls, she hadn't left me a voicemail at all. If anything, she probably was worried that I hadn't pick up the phone or called her right back like I usually do. I could already feel she was going to have a major attitude when I got home, so I took the rest of the drive in silence, hoping I would be able to be calm enough to deal with her messed up mood when I got home.

When I pulled up to the house, her car was parked in its usual spot and Marisol's Toyota Camry was gone which meant she had sent her home for the evening. I parked my truck and then walked into the house through the kitchen. I found Denise upstairs in our bedroom sitting on our bed flipping through channels on T.V. and Kaylah was lying next to her, sleeping peacefully like my princess always does. I leaned down and kissed Kaylah on her little chubby cheek and although my kiss caused her to stir, she remained sleep. I smiled as I watched her for a few seconds.

Denise sat where she was and continued to flip through channels like she didn't even see me come in the room. So since she didn't plan on saying anything, I figured I would take the first step.

"Hey baby. I missed you. How's my number one lady doing?" I asked her as I bent down and tried to kiss her, but she turned her face so I ended up catching her cheek.

"Hey, babe, did you know that I called you?"

"Yeah, I know you called me. I think you called like ten times. I didn't have my phone close to me when you were trying to reach me. What's up?" I asked.

"Well, nothing now. I guess it doesn't matter now. If you know I called you that many times, then why didn't you bother calling me back? It could've been an emergency for crying out loud. And since when don't you have your phone on you? It's usually always on your holster clip on your hip. Where were you?"

"You know where I was. I was at the church all day where I usually am, and then I stopped over Momma's for a little while."

"I called the church when you were supposed to be there and you didn't answer and then when I called Mama Alice, she said you had left her house over an hour ago."

"When I left mom's house, I ran into Alexis and she needed help with moving around a few things so I helped her and then I came straight home. I ended up leaving my phone in the car the entire time I was at Mom's so that's why you weren't able to reach me. I'm sorry babe. I won't do that ever again." I explained and then reached down to kiss her. She gave me a quick kiss. I could tell she wanted to say way more; but instead just ended what she was going to say with a kiss. I'll take one of those over an argument any day.

"Eww, you're so sweaty. Please go and wash your funkiness...please," she said as she plugged up her nose with her fingers. All I could do was laugh.

"Yes, ma'am. I'm going to do that right away."

I was so glad that my wife didn't choose to argue with me about helping Alexis, especially since we had just gotten over arguing about her anyway. She must've really heard from the Lord about picking and choosing her battles and I was surely thankful.

HOLY REVENGE

I walked into the bathroom and turned the shower on while I got myself ready. If there was one thing that I truly loved about my house, I would have to say it would be my bathroom and its ability to isolate me from the rest of the world so I could relax. It didn't matter what kind of day I had, by the time I was done showering I had a smile on my face.

By the time I opened the glass door to the shower the water was nice, hot, and steamy just like I like it. I stepped in and allowed the water jets to hit me from both sides of the double shower head I had installed and it felt so good. I closed my eyes and allowed the shower and my thoughts to take me away.

As I continued to relax, that's when a vision of her appeared. Her back was turned to me so I couldn't see her face, but from behind I could tell it was my wife. Perfectly manicured toes that I could see myself tasting; long beautiful legs that always had the ability to turn me on; and beautiful caramel skin that was as smooth as chocolate.

She was dressed in a silk teddy and matching robe which I removed and let fall to the floor. I kissed the edge of her shoulder and closed my eyes taking in the sweet scent of her perfume which had intoxicating effects on me. I planted small kisses on her back and I couldn't believe how much I missed her. I moved up to her neck and then began kissing the spot right behind her left ear. I knew this gesture would drive her crazy and went further in to kiss her again until I heard,

"That's it *Junior*...right there!" When the woman turned around I realized that it was not Denise, it was Alexis! She is the only one that has *ever* called me Junior. She was the fantasy woman that had caused me to get so aroused. My eyes popped open and I snapped out of my little daydream. I looked around and realized I was still alone in the bathroom.

Whew! That was definitely a close one. I could've sworn that the woman that I was fantasizing about was Denise. I never imagined it would be Alexis. I couldn't believe my mind had drifted off like it just did. Wow...I really need to pray that I don't have any more dreams like that about Alexis, and I definitely need to pray that my friend ceases his *excitement* by the time I'm done in the bathroom.

HOLY REVENGE

Even though Denise and I are best friends and have a lot of differences, there is one thing in which we are a united front in and that's in our dislike for Daphne. I don't know what it is about that woman that irritates me, but somehow, someway, she has the capability of getting all up underneath my skin. I arrived at Oakdale Baptist a little earlier than I expected but I wasn't complaining. At least I had finally made it to church. I figured I would find Denise and we could catch up for a few minutes. I texted her while I was parking my car, to see where she was and she told me she was in the sanctuary so as soon as I found a parking spot that's the exact direction I went in.

Yeah, I know you're real surprised to hear me speak of going to church but I do go...just not all of the time. I know that may sound horrible to you avid church attendees, but with a schedule like I have as one of the most prominent and in demand lawyers of the city, I'm lucky if I even able to schedule in sleeping or eating. Lately my schedule has been so crazy that I've barely been able to catch up, let alone make time to spend with Carlos, but I've been trying my hardest to do better. Carlos has been helping me to stop and take time to just enjoy life, and I'm so glad he's in my life, otherwise I'd probably be working myself to death. Now the only thing I really need to improve on is my church attendance and then I'll be just fine.

Besides, if my mother calls me one more time and asks me why I missed Sunday service, I think I'm going to scream. So I beat her to the punch. Instead of being woke up to her calling me super early on Sunday and asking me why I was neglecting the Lord Almighty; my Savior, I set my alarm clock early, and by the time the phone was ringing I answered it singing Amazing Grace. One of the hymns she used to sing to me all the time when I was a little girl. That completely messed her up, and by the time I had finished the end of the verse she was in tears.

I thought I was going to give her a heart attack when I told her I would be in service today. She immediately began to break out into a cry and her Holy-Ghost tongue. Even though I know my mother can be a little over the top sometimes, I knew she was right about a lot of things. I do need to be back in church on the regular, and that was the exact reason why I had made it my mission to go today. I knew I had to start somewhere and baby steps are better than no steps at all.

Once I made it into the sanctuary, that's when I saw the one person I didn't want to see...Daphne. I swear if I could, I would've walked straight up to her and punched her right in her face. But I couldn't do that, and it definitely wasn't my style at all, even though I was tempted in the worst way. I think everyone in the church wanted to knock her upside her head and wipe off that stupid Christian grin that she wore on her face, but we all did what we had to do to keep our cool.

I watched her as she walked around and spoke to different people carrying her Bible underneath her arm as though it was her clutch purse. The sight of her made me want to gag, but I refrained from doing just that. I walked down the center aisle until I reached the front of the church where Denise and Kaylah were, and then Daphne made her way over to me as well.

"So Terri...it's so good to see you this Sunday." She said as she offered that same stupid smile that was a source of irritation to me.

Jessica A. Robinson

"It's good to see you too." I answered her knowing I had just told a bold face lie. But let's be honest, how many times have you lied in someone's face you didn't want to see?

"I'm glad you *finally* are making time for the Lord. Don't think because you're some big attorney making all that money that you don't have to make time for the things of God, because you do. He'll take it all away in a heartbeat when we think too highly of ourselves." Daphne said, and continued walking until she found her seat.

"What is wrong with her? I asked Denise as I took a seat next to her and sat down. Kaylah was making noise and smiling at me so I picked her up out of her car seat and held her.

"I don't know Terri. I ask myself that question almost every day." She laughed and then gave me a hug.

"It's so good to see you here. It's definitely been a while."

"Yes, it has but I'm trying to do better. Besides you know how my mother can be. She is relentless about me attending church on the regular."

"So I know she's happy about you being here today."

"Ecstatic! She'll probably be shouting up and down the aisle before service is over. Something tells me a Holy-Ghost dance will be done today." I laugh at my own joke.

"You are hilarious. How have you been?"

"I've been okay. Been swamped at work, but what's new; I'm always busy. Carlos and I are okay, but I just have some questions about a phone call I heard him on the other day."

"Why? What happened?"

"Well, he came to pick me up and he went downstairs to wait for me, when I came down he was on the phone arguing with someone and I didn't hear much, but he told the woman to lose his number and to leave him alone."

"How did you know it was a woman?"

"Because I heard him call her name...*Estella* and after he got off the phone with her, he was in such a bad mood for the entire night. And when I asked him what was wrong with him he told me a bill collector had called him and gotten him upset." I replied.

"A bill collector made him that mad? I don't know, but that doesn't sound right to me."

"I said the same exact thing. I don't care how many bill collectors call me, I'm not going to let them get me upset, and I'm sure I don't know them on a first name basis."

"Right. Well maybe you should talk to him and get to the bottom of it."

"I want to, but if I bring this up to him about what I heard, he's going to know that I eavesdropped on his conversation, and I know he'll be mad because he's gonna feel like I don't trust him."

"I see what you mean. Yeah, well in that case I wouldn't bring it up to him because you do want to trust him, but if I were you I would file that name, 'Estella' in my memory bank because you know God always has a way of bringing things back around to you."

Before I could answer, I heard the minister of music start playing music and the worship team came up on stage and started their first song. I kissed my god child and handed her back to Denise.

"What are you doing later?" She whispered right before I could walk away.

"Nothing. Why what's up?"

"Well, come over later. I'm cooking dinner."

"I'll be there." I said, as I walked away and sat in my usual spot right near the back of the church. I know with Denise being my best friend and all, I could easily have the best seat in the house right in the front on the first row, but that's too much pressure if you ask me. I don't like sitting up front at all; not one bit. Everyone stares at you, and it seems like all their eyes focus in on you at once. You can't see anyone else who walks in unless you turn your head and make it obvious that you're trying to be nosy. I'm a nosy person, but I don't want everyone and their mama knowing that. Also being up front makes you really have to pay attention to what the minister is saying because when they feel like they need a little extra help they do not hesitate in calling you out in front of everyone. That's exactly why I hate sitting up front.

I would love to sit next to my best friend and chat with her all service long, but not under those conditions. I like sitting in the back. It's close to the bathrooms in case I really have to go, it's close to the exit in case I need to leave in a hurry, and I can slip in and slip out at my convenience without anyone being all up in my business.

Some of the members complain about having to sit in the back if they come late and there aren't any closer seats, but I don't complain at all. Sitting in the back is actually my area of preference. Just before the praise team was done singing, my mother made her way to the end of her row and down the left outer aisle and came back to where I was seated.

"Baby it's so good to see you in church. Daddy says 'hello' as well."

"It's good to be here mom. Thanks for staying on me. I appreciate it."

"If you don't have any plans later, you can come over for dinner. Your dad and I would like to finally meet Carlos."

"Aww mom, I'm sorry but I already have plans, but I promise you and dad will meet him soon." I smiled.

"Okay, baby, I'll see you later." My mother said and then she walked back to her seat and sat down.

It's amazing to me that I'm so close to forty years old, and my mother still checks up on me as

HOLY REVENGE

though I were a teenager. I guess since I am the only child, that they're trying to make that moment last forever, but I'm sorry to tell them, that moment has come and gone. But they wouldn't be my parents if they didn't feel the need to watch me close.

Right after the offering, I decided I would make my exit and leave. I gathered my things quietly, and walked through the lobby to the front doors of the church.

"Have a wonderful day Ms. Terri." Kenny, the security guard said as he winked and switched the toothpick he was sucking on to the opposite side of his mouth.

"You too." I pressed my lips together and offered a polite smile.

I didn't really care for Kenny too much. I don't even know why, but there was something about him that I didn't like. Maybe it was because I felt like he was super sneaky and really didn't do his job like I think he should. To me, it seemed like he did more people watching, than securing the premises and making sure everyone was safe. I know I'm not at church a lot, so who am I to complain, but I'm just simply sharing my observation. Kenny always seems to be busy doing nothing.

I left out of the church feeling good that I pressed my way to actually come. After Randy preached Heaven down to earth, and I heard good music, I was ready to eat some of my best friend's great cooking. I started weaving through the first set of cars in the parking lot to make my way to my car when I noticed there was something attached to the front windshield of Randy and Denise's truck.

I scanned the parking lot and noticed that no one else had a note on their car except them. I was going to keep going and just leave the note there, but against my better judgment, I walked over, lifted the windshield wiper up, and retrieved the note.

Jessica A. Robinson

I looked around to see if anyone was watching me before I walked to my car and left. Once I pulled out the parking lot, I immediately got caught by a red light. While I waited for the light to turn green, I picked up the note that I had laid on the passenger's seat and flipped it over to inspect it. The note was addressed to Denise but someone used magazine letters to spell her name out instead of writing her name on the envelope. I don't know, but the more and more I looked at the envelope, something about it just wasn't right.

I decided against opening the note even though I wanted to see what was inside so bad. I figured Denise would tell me what the note said anyway. I glanced down at my watch and saw that it was still early enough to stop by and see Carlos before he went to work. I smiled wide as I pulled onto his street and saw his white pick-up truck parked in the driveway. I used the key he gave me, and let myself in and heard him in the living room talking on his cell phone. I swear that man couldn't live without his phone. When he saw me, he walked up to me, gave me a quick kiss and then continued on with his conversation.

He walked over to the coffee table and gathered up a stack of papers and stuffed them inside a manila envelope. He took the envelope and walked upstairs and shut his bedroom door. I don't know if it was just me, but Carlos seemed to be real secretive lately, and I didn't have the slightest clue why. I flipped through the *Black Enterprise* magazine that graced his end table and almost as soon as I opened the book Carlos was making his way back downstairs, minus the phone and the envelope.

"Hey baby. How are you? I missed you." Carlos walked over and wrapped me in his arms. I leaned into him and kissed him softly like I always did.

"I missed you too."

"How was church?"

HOLY REVENGE

"It was great. Randy preached a great message. I really enjoyed myself. You should come with me next time."

"You know what? I think I'll take you up on your offer. I like going to church, I just haven't been in forever."

"Me too. I'm always too swamped with work to go, and by the looks of it, you're just as busy as me. You sure do have a lot of paperwork to complete." I said letting him know that I saw the stack of papers that he was so desperately trying to hide from me. I didn't get a good look at what any of those documents were saying, but I did get the feeling that he didn't want me to see them.

"Oh, you're talking about all those papers that were on the coffee table? Oh, that's nothing babe. I'll finish all of that stuff up later on when I get back home."

"So you still have to work today?" I asked.

"Yeah, actually I was just getting ready to leave out in a few. I probably won't get done until ten or eleven. What are your plans for the rest of the day?"

"I was just invited to dinner, so I'm going over Denise and Randy's. I can always save you a plate and you can eat tomorrow."

"That sounds great. I would like that." Carlos replied, and then looked down at his watch.

"Okay, honey well, I gotta get going, but we'll hook up at some point tomorrow. Have a good time and tell your friends I said 'hello', I can't wait to meet them." Carlos gave me another hug and a kiss and we walked out of his house together. So he had managed to change the subject for a second time and was acting completely weird. I don't understand, but one thing I did do was piece things together; *that's what lawyers do*. I was going to get to the bottom of this some way or somehow.

I drove home, changed my clothes, and was at Denise's house within an hour.

"That was fast. We just got home like twenty minutes ago." Denise said, as she opened up her front door to let me in.

"Well, I ended up leaving church early so I could see my man before he went to work and then I went home for an hour."

"It seem like church wasn't ever going to end. After offering, Sister Honey wanted to get up and give a testimony, but you know that woman can talk and never shuts up, so we were in church forever, while she retold her story three different times in a new way trying to get people to shout and fall out because of her words. I felt like getting up and walking out, but you know that isn't proper as a pastor's wife." Denise said, as she talked with her fake British accent and I busted out laughing.

"I surely did leave at a great time."

"Yes, you sure did."

"Hey, where's Randy at?" I asked, as I shut the door behind me and locked it.

"He's down the hall in his study catching up on the game he missed the other day, why what's up?"

"Well, I wanted to go upstairs and raid your closet and see what new things I can steal, I mean borrow." I replied.

"Oh, come on girl, let's go up and see." Denise said, as she started going upstairs and I followed right behind her. When we got in her bedroom, I shut the door behind me and Denise continued to the closet. She walked to her expansive walk-in-closet and turned the light on.

"I just purchased all new things for the conference and besides that, I got a few other things sent to me in the mail from one of my stylists I work with from time to time, so you can come in here and check it all out." She announced.

"Denise, I didn't want to come up and look at any clothes, but I did want to come up here and talk though."

HOLY REVENGE

"What's up?" Denise asked. I pulled the weird note out of my purse and handed it to her.

"When I left church today, I saw this attached to the windshield of your truck."

I sat quietly as Denise took the note from me and opened it up. She sat the envelope it was in down and then read the note aloud.

Denise,

No matter where you go or what you do, know that I am watching you. So watch your step, I'm watching your every move little miss perfect.

"You don't know who would've sent that to you?" I asked, as she passed the note to me and I looked at it.

"I have no clue. I don't even know what they're talking about."

"Do you think someone is following you?"

"I doubt it. I think whoever it is, is just trying to harass me that's all. Ever since this stuff with Tyrone, people have been doing little stupid things trying to scare me; but I don't pay it, or them, any attention."

"Have you told Randy or the police?"

"I haven't told the police, but Randy knows of a few things like people calling and playing on my phone, but that has stopped for the most part. It's sad to say, but I think it's one of the jealous women that go to our church who has nothing better to do with their time than to bother me.

"Well, I think you should tell him and the police about this note. This could be serious." I said as I handed the note back to her. She folded the note up and then proceeded to rip it up into a whole bunch of pieces.

"Why are you ripping it up Denise?"

"Because I'm going to throw it away; I don't need Randy finding the note and flipping out for that matter. It's fine, just a few haters trying to be funny. I'm not worried in the least bit at all." Denise replied,

Jessica A. Robinson

and then noticed that her *Blackberry* was buzzing with a private number.

"Who's that Denise?" I asked.

"It says private; hold on." Denise lifted the phone up to her ear and pressed 'answer'.

"Hello." She waited for the person won the other end of the phone to say something, but all she heard was their breathing.

Before Denise could say anything else, the line went dead. She placed the phone back on the nightstand where it previously was.

"I don't know who it was because they never said anything; they probably had the wrong number." She offered a smile and shrugged it off as if it was mere coincidence, but the fact that Denise heard the person on the other end of the phone breathing made me think otherwise.

"So, they've stopped playing on your phone huh?" I said as I raised my eyebrows and smacked my lips.

"I don't think anyone is playing on my phone. People do dial wrong phone numbers ya know? Anyways enough about me...how about we host the dinner party for you and Carlos the week after the conference. That will give us more than enough time to prepare and to make it really nice for you two and you can invite your parents as well." I smiled from ear to ear at the mention of his name. It caused Denise to snicker.

"Okay, I'm too excited. I can't wait for you all to finally meet. He's excited to meet you all too."

I was glad I'd finally found a man that made me happy enough that I wanted to take him to meet my friends and family. I was excited for Randy and Denise to meet him because I knew they would like him, but I was nervous for my parents to finally meet him. In their book, no one would ever be good enough for me.

"I like how you changed the subject on me all fast and everything, but please hear me out; be careful.

HOLY REVENGE

You and I both know how crazy people can be. We've seen it first-hand. I know you've changed your life for the better, but watch what you're doing because there's always someone in the background waiting for your downfall."

"You are so right. Don't worry, I'm being careful. I've learned my lesson." Denise took the shredded pieces of paper and threw them directly in the trash. I really hoped my friend was telling me the complete truth. Sometimes she had the worst habit of withholding certain pieces of information from me because she said that I tend to blow situations up bigger than they should be, but I beg to differ. She's so nonchalant with everything that she can blow the most serious of situations off, and sometimes I have to remind her of just how serious things are.

I had a feeling that my best friend wasn't telling me the complete truth. If I knew her like I thought I knew her, there were definitely some bits and pieces that she had neglected to tell me, but all I could hold on to was the hope and assurance that she really had changed for the better, because if she was still doing some sneaky things behind the scenes, God only knows what would transpire this time.

Chapter 7 (Denise)

I was in my King-sized bed, getting some great sleep, when I heard my husband calling my name. I almost didn't want to wake up, but I decided against ignoring him altogether. I figured I would at least stay asleep until he called me again.

"Denise, wake up baby." Randy called out again causing me to yawn and open my eyes. When I finally opened my eyes I discovered it was Tyrone who had been calling me instead of my husband! I jumped out of bed and tripped over a pair of shoes that Randy had sitting next to the bed. I got up as fast as I could.

"How did you get here? We buried you. You're supposed to be..." I couldn't even finish my last sentence because the sight of him had me so speechless.

"What? I'm supposed to be *dead*...but guess what? I can never die. You thought you could just do whatever you wanted with me and then throw me away like I was nothing, but you've got another thing coming. I'm back and I'm ready to take you with me!"

Tyrone lifted a gun from behind his back, aimed it at my head, and pulled the trigger. I screamed out at the top of my lungs. I sprang out of bed and realized that I'd just had one of the most horrible dreams in my life. My sudden reaction caused Randy to be jolted from his sleep.

"Baby, what's wrong? What's going on?" He asked as he sat up in bed and looked over at me.

"I'm okay, I just need to go and check on the baby." I answered as I got out of the bed and hurried down the hallway to the nursery where Kaylah was. Thank God, she was still sound asleep and hadn't heard anything at all. I didn't wake her. I walked out of her room leaving the door semi open just in case she did wake up. I walked back into our bedroom and saw my husband sitting on the side of the bed, not knowing whether he was coming or going. I know my sudden scream had completely disturbed his sleep, but I had never had this happen to me before.

"Okay, Denise you're scaring me. What's going on?" Randy asked as he got up and wrapped his arms around me.

"I'm sorry I startled you baby; but I'm fine."

"I know you're saying you're fine, but what's going on? You know you can talk to me about whatever it is that's bothering you."

For a moment, I thought about not saying anything about the nightmare I just had, but if there was any person I could talk to, I know it was my husband.

"I had a nightmare. I dreamed that Tyrone had come into our house trying to kill me." I replied and then put my head down. I hated bringing up his name in our house. Tyrone's name definitely brought a sour mood when it was mentioned, so I tried to say his name as least as possible.

Randy hugged me tight and rubbed my back.

"I'm sorry you dreamt that. You don't have to worry about that crazy fool ever coming to hurt you at all. He's gone; for good." Randy said, as he stroked my hair and I began to cry. He wiped my tears with his hand and then began to kiss me softly.

"I know he's gone for good, but the dream I had just seemed so real. I've never had a dream like that. It was just crazy."

"Listen to me. That part of our lives is over. He was a disturbed man. I've had a few dreams like that before. I've even had a few where I dreamt we were in church on the day of Kaylah's christening when Tyrone came up in church waving a gun just like he did that day, so I know exactly how you feel." He explained. I never knew Randy even had any dreams like the one I just had. It just makes me feel so horrible when I think about all of the pain I've caused him; all because of my own stupidity.

"I'm so sorry Randy. I wish I could turn back the hand of time and take all the wrong I've done back." I said as I continued to cry.

"Baby, it's okay. No one ever said this life would be easy. There are going to be some things that we have to deal with and move on and this is one of those moments. We can't continue to live in the past, what's important now is that we continue to move forward."

"You're right."

"And by the looks of the clock over there, if you don't get a move on it, you'll be late in getting to the airport to pick up your guest speaker for the conference." Randy smiled as he wiped the last of my tears away and kissed me.

"Yeah, I better get going. I wouldn't want to keep her waiting." I said, as I went into the bathroom and started my shower. If Myra would've just accepted the fact that our transportation department would be picking her up then she would have a ride from the airport already. I counted it to be such an inconvenience to stop everything that I was doing just so that I could drive to the airport to pick her up. If you ask me, I think she's a diva, and if that's the case then I was definitely going to have a problem with her because there was only one diva at Oakdale; and that was ME!

After I got myself ready, Randy decided that he would stay and see about Kaylah, which was such a big help to me because it allowed me to leave earlier so I would miss the morning traffic. I looked in my car for the email confirmations for her flight and her hotel, but I couldn't find them anywhere. I searched the glove compartment, the trunk, and my purse. They weren't

HOLY REVENGE

anywhere. I'd forgotten that I left all of those emails on the receptionist desk at the church. Even though I didn't want to drive to the church, I knew I would be completely lost without the information so I had to stop by there first.

When I got down to the church and pulled in the parking lot, I saw Kenny's busted-up Pacer sitting in its usual spot looking nothing short of depressed. I rolled my eyes at the fact that I would have to interact with him today. It was true that Oakdale was the largest mega church in the city of Youngstown, but with our head security guard having cameras that covered every facet of the church, he made it his duty to know exactly where I was at all times when I was there. I walked past his little sad car and laughed as I walked inside of the church. I know Randy paid him a good salary to work here at our ministry, I couldn't understand for the life of me why he didn't upgrade his transportation?

I couldn't even walk down the steps good enough before Kenny was there at the top opening the door for me like he was the bellhop.

"To what do I owe this honor?" Kenny asked as he moved to the side so that I could step through the door.

"I don't owe you anything Kenny; I was coming here because I forgot something." I answered as I tried my best to walk past him and keep it moving to get what I needed, but knowing him, he wouldn't let me go that easily.

"I knew you wanted to see me bad today, I could feel it." Kenny said as he followed me down the hall until I reached the receptionist desk. I didn't pay him any mind, just continued to look through documents on the desk until I found what I needed.

"Kenny, please stop the foolishness. I didn't come here to see you; I came to get what I needed so that I can pick our speaker up this afternoon. That's all."

"I'm not playing any games at all. You're the one who insists on playing games with me. You know I want you and what's funny is I know you want me too. I can feel it."

"Come on please..." I laughed as I continued on with what I was doing; not even noticing he had moved in so close to me that I couldn't move until it was too late.

"Like I said I know you want me. I can see it in your eyes and the way you look at me every time you see me or say something to me. You're just in denial, but I'm not anymore." Kenny replied as he leaned in and planted a kiss smack dab on my lips.

He pulled back and stared at me with the sexy glare that he's always given me since day one. I couldn't even deny the fact that this man was indeed sexy. He was really an annoying presence in my life, but he was definitely sexy, and the way he always took charge and his persistence was a turn on to me, but Kenny was off limits. He was employed, first and foremost by my husband, and messing with him on any level would be a dangerous move on my behalf. And the last thing I needed was to be caught up in some more drama in the church. I had caused enough drama already.

"I can't believe you just did that. Kenny, you were way out of line with that and you know it." I replied, as I wiped his kiss away from my mouth in disgust.

"I admit, I may have caught you off guard, but was I out of line?" Kenny asked as he still remained close to me.

"Yes, you were out of line. Are you crazy?"

"No, I'm not crazy. I just want you; that's all."

"You're obviously crazy. Kissing me like that when you know good and well this is the worst place to do something like that and there's cameras all around. I really can't believe you." I said as I made sure I lowered my voice. I didn't need any of the church members who

HOLY REVENGE

were in the church to conjure up any gossip because they thought they seen or heard something.

"Don't worry about any cameras. You think I would really be that stupid and incriminate myself when I work here too? There aren't cameras in this area, so chill. I know you enjoyed the kiss even though you're trying to act all irritated." Kenny said. I shook my head 'no' and crossed my arms.

"Tell me you didn't enjoy the kiss." Kenny said.

"I didn't enjoy the kiss Kenny. You were wrong and you know it." I explained and put my head down trying to get a hold of myself. The honest truth was his kiss had set me on fire!

I hoped Kenny would just take me for my word and wouldn't decide to probe any further into my response, but he did.

"I beg to differ. I think you did like the kiss. You're just playing hard to get, that's all."

"Well, I'm not playing hard to get. I love my husband and you were wrong for coming at me this way, and now, if you'll excuse me, I need to get going." I said, as I grabbed the last of the documents off the desk and walked as fast as I could down the hallway and out of the church. I had to get out of there as fast as I could before I turned around and did some things to him that I would have to lie on the altar and ask for forgiveness about afterward. I hadn't had sex in so long that a kiss like the one he just gave me made me want to strip right then and there, and worry about everything else later.

Even though I felt he was completely out of line for what he just did, there was still a tiny part of me that was turned on by his rude-boy behavior. It was spontaneous moments like that which caused a small fire to wage within me; but I immediately started to pray. I had to pray to stop these feelings and thoughts, because if I didn't, they would definitely skip an inch and take a mile until they took over me.

Jessica A. Robinson

As soon as I shut my car door, before I even pulled off, I said a small prayer: *Lord, please take away these feelings I'm experiencing for that sexy man; in Jesus name, Amen.*

Kenny exhibited the same type of qualities that made Tyrone so irresistible to me. The take charge—you're all mine—attitude that Kenny had shown me made him very sexy. Even though I was attracted to Kenny sexually, I wasn't trying to fall into temptation with him. Going through all of the drama with Tyrone had, in fact, cured me from any previous desire that I had to step out on Randy. It made me stronger, and I wasn't trying to travel down that familiar road with anyone else again. I'd learned my lesson. Coming so close to death had that type of effect on me.

I pulled onto the interstate and popped in Beyonce's, *Sasha Fierce* CD and allowed her catchy lyrics and powerful voice to carry me all the way to Cleveland. My cell phone started to ring just as I was exiting the Ohio Turnpike. I wasn't going to answer it, but when I saw 'Danielle' flash across the screen. I decided to press the green button.

"Hey Darnell. How are you?" I asked as I turned on my *Bluetooth* so I could talk and drive at the same time.

"I'm great. Thanks for asking. I'm surprised I even got you on the phone. I've been hearing about the big women's conference your church is having this week."

"Yeah, it's gonna be a pretty busy week, but I'm not complaining. So what's up?"

"Well, I didn't want to bother you, but I was calling you to see whether or not you thought about meeting up with me. I would really like an opportunity to speak with you in person if that's okay with you."

"Um, I don't know about that Darnell. I promised my husband that I would have no contact with any of Tyrone's family members and I'm really trying to keep my word. I don't blame you for anything that's happened, but I made Randy that promise so..."

HOLY REVENGE

"I understand, but there are some things that I really need to talk with you about in person, and over the phone just won't do. I don't want you to break your promise to your husband or nothing like that, but if you could meet with me at some point I would greatly appreciate it."

What part of, "I don't really think meeting with you at any point is a good idea" don't he understand?

"Darnell, I gotta go right now, someone is calling on my other line, but if I meet up with you, it has to be sometime next week and no one must know about this. This cannot get back to my husband." I explained.

"Don't worry; I won't say anything at all. I'll just call you at some point next week and we can meet out somewhere."

"Okay Darnell, talk to you then."

I pulled up to the gate where Myra was supposed to be and waited for her to emerge. I had never seen her face to face. I'd only seen a few pictures of her on the Internet and the pictures I'd seen revealed a tall, large woman. So I had an idea of what Myra looked like, but I wasn't sure how current the pictures I'd seen were. I waited for what seemed like hours for Myra to come out and was honestly getting ready to leave her for taking so long, but just when I was going to turn on my car and pull off, a woman approached my car.

"Hello, are you Denise Tate?" The tall, thin woman leaned down and asked.

"Yes, are you Myra?" I asked pressing the button to pop my trunk.

"Yes, I am. It's so nice to finally meet you." She smiled. I got out of my Benz and walked around to the side where she was standing. For a brief second, I took in her appearance before Myra broke the ice and extended her arms out to hug me. Myra looked nothing like her pictures. In the pictures that were posted on her website, she looked to be close to a size eighteen and the woman standing before me looked to be no bigger than a size six. Instead of being a plus size woman, Myra looked like she could be a model! She was very tall, almost six feet; with long flowing hair that touched the middle of her back. Her skin was smooth and flawless and she had a very beautiful white smile. She looked like she could be on somebody's runway; she was so pretty. I didn't care how beautiful she was, she still couldn't hold a candle to me even on her best day.

"It's so great to finally meet you. And thank you for coming to pick me up from the airport."

"It's no problem at all. Thank you for coming to be a part of our conference." I opened up my trunk all the way and signaled for the man who was carrying Myra's luggage to place the items in the car.

"It's my pleasure Mrs. Tate."

"Oh, call me Denise." I smiled and we both got into the car at the same time.

"I must say you look very different from the pictures you have on your website." I remarked.

Myra smiled and then let out a slight laugh. "I know those pictures look nothing like me. They're about two years old. It's hard to believe that I used to be that size; but God is good, I needed to lose some weight, initially for my health, but God took over and allowed me to lose so much more."

I nodded. I must say I was impressed at the dramatic change in Myra. When Daphne had first showed me what she looked like, I couldn't help but think the woman looked like a taller version of a fat oompa loompa from the *Wizard of Oz*.

"Well, congratulations, you look great." I replied. I pulled my car out of park and then drove away. I was well onto the interstate before Myra said anything else.

"I want to thank you for agreeing to come and get me from the airport. I know you may have found my request somewhat odd, but everything I do is for a reason."

HOLY REVENGE

"And that reason is?"

"When I go to a ministry for the first time, I would like to meet with the Pastor and First Lady and since this is a woman's conference, I thought it was fitting to meet you first."

"Okay."

I was getting ready to say something else when my CD player spontaneously turned on and started playing the music I was previously listening to. I was beyond embarrassed.

"Woman of God, I'm sorry about that. My brother-in-law was driving my car and I have to always get on him about listening to those secular CD's while he's in here." I smiled and Myra nodded.

"It's okay. I totally understand; you don't have to explain anything to me. I have Beyonce on repeat as well on my iPod." Myra smiled politely and I smiled back at her. Even though she admitted to listening to some of the same kinds of music I was still embarrassed to say the least.

As I drove, I couldn't figure out how my CD player turned on after I distinctly remembered turning it off before I got out of the car. But then again my CD player did act funny sometimes and seem to have a mind of its own at times. I made a mental note to get it checked out at the Benz dealership when I had some free time.

During the drive to Myra's hotel, we made small talk about the conference and I was glad I'd followed through with booking her for our event. At first, when Daphne had recommended Myra Washington during one of our planning meetings, I told her I had never heard of her which was the truth because I hadn't heard of the woman until Daphne introduced her. I then asked Daphne how she'd previously heard of Myra and she said Kenny had suggested that she be one of the speakers. Since I didn't trust a word Kenny said, I decided to research the suggestion myself and after catching a few of her *YouTube* videos and looking through her website, I determined that she would be a perfect fit for what we were trying to do.

I had to give personal recognition and thanks to Daphne and Kenny, because Myra's captivating presence and personality caused her to deliver some of the most powerful messages I ever heard come from a woman. I knew that Myra Washington was sure to be a hit with the women of our congregation.

Before I knew it, I was already making a right hand turn into the Embassy Hotel, and I pulled directly under the carport where there was a bellhop waiting for us.

"Well, here we are." I announced. I opened my trunk and went out to meet the bellman. After he had loaded all of her luggage onto the cart, I reached inside my pocket and handed Myra her room keys.

"Here's your room keys; everything is already taken care of. There's even a special gift in your room as our way to say, 'thank you'."

Myra reached out and hugged me.

"Thank you so much. I really appreciate everything." She turned and started walking toward the entrance of the building. I called out to her just before she walked through the sliding glass doors.

"If you need anything, please don't hesitate to call me."

Okay, you can call me soft, or whatever you would like but my first impression of Myra was a pleasant one, and to that I was pleasantly surprised. It's not too often that you run into a high-profile speaker like Myra who is actually humble and down to earth. I had a good feeling about her being a part of the conference.

When I finally made it home, I found Randy in his den with Kaylah lying on his chest. He was watching some action movie and she was somewhere in sleepy land counting sheep. The sight of the two of them caused me to smile wide. Even though he wasn't her actual biological father, you could see the bond between them.

Before I could say anything to Randy, my phone began to vibrate, which caused me to slightly jump because I wasn't expecting it.

"Hello." I said. Once again the person on the other end of the phone said nothing, but I could hear them breathing like they did the last time they called. Instead of entertaining their foolishness, I hung up. I shook my head and then sighed. Randy put Kaylah down on the couch and then greeted me with a kiss.

"Who was that baby?"

"I don't know. It was probably a wrong number." I answered, and then stuffed my phone back inside my purse.

"Denise you smell like men's cologne. Where have you been?" Randy asked me as the thoughts about being around Kenny popped back into my mind.

"Oh, um, when I was at the airport the guy that was helping us load Myra's luggage had an incredibly large amount of cologne on and after he was done helping us he left his scent on me, Myra, and her luggage." I laughed hoping that Randy would believe me.

"Wow, that's crazy. Well, I can't figure out what he was wearing, but I know it definitely has to be cheap by the way it smells." He smiled.

Randy was right about one thing. The cologne he smelled on me was definitely cheap because of who was wearing it, but what he didn't know was who the cheap ass cologne actually belonged to. Kenny had been so close to me on more than one occasion that I could spot his cologne a mile away.

"So, tell me what was your first impression of Myra? Is she nice?" He asked.

"Actually she's very nice, which completely caught me off guard because I wasn't expecting that at all. I believe she's a good fit for our conference."

"Good, that's what I like to hear."

Jessica A. Robinson

"So what have you and Kaylah been doing all day since I've been gone?"

"After I gave her a bath and got her dressed, we played for a little while; I fed her, and then put her down for a nap. And while she was sleep I had a phone meeting with Minister Mason Chilton, the man of God from Trinity Fellowship that I'm trying to add to our staff."

"Well, how did that go?"

"We had a nice phone conversation, but the things I was saying to him fell on deaf ears. He wasn't swayed at all."

"Did you mention that you would also put him on salary too?" I asked.

"Yes, I told him everything that we were offering him and that still didn't move him at all."

"I wonder why he would turn down such an offer." I asked even though I could probably figure out the reason why he didn't want to accept such a wonderful offer.

"No. I guess he just wasn't interested. It's okay honey, God will lead us to the right person for the job when it's time."

My husband had such a decent way of looking at things, but I wasn't stupid, nor was I born yesterday. I knew exactly why Mason Chilton didn't want the job. It was because of all of the drama and scandal surrounding my affair. Even though our church was the premiere church to attend in the city, there still was a level of uncertainty when it came to outside people and visitors who had heard of the recent events that had taken place at our ministry. And I couldn't blame them at all.

The things that had taken place at Oakdale sounded like they could be on the front page of every major magazine; and believe me it made headlines in some of the online bloggers and gossip magazines, but we had paid a pretty penny to our publicist to do what they call, "damage control" and it was money well invested. Other than a few of those sites posting fabricated and juiced up stories anyway, we had done a great job in making sure that the drama didn't remain in the media too long.

I knew Randy probably didn't want to tell me exactly what Mason said about why he didn't want to become a part of our ministerial staff because he didn't want to hurt my feelings and that was fine with me.

"You're right Randy. I believe you won't have to wait much longer. The right person for the position will be drawn to the ministry before you know it. I pray that even now, that God is preparing someone who will step up to the plate, and that they will be a perfect fit." I embraced him trying my best to reassure him not to worry.

"Thanks baby. That's why I love you and I truly believe what you just said." Randy bent down and kissed me again which only caused me to want to do one thing: I wanted to take him by the hand and lead him upstairs just so that I could show him how much I really did love him, but knowing Randy, he would just make up some dumb excuse as to why he didn't want to have sex. I guess I would have to take his words of wisdom and be patient. *Everything in God's timing*, is the phrase that kept ringing in my head for the rest of the day. I desperately hoped that God's timing was on point, because I could feel myself getting to a point where if things didn't change in our sex life, then I don't know what I might be capable of.

"**G**ood afternoon everyone. First and foremost, my husband and I would like to welcome you to our kickoff luncheon for our first annual women's conference. You could be anywhere else in the world at this moment, but we're so glad to have you are here taking part in this special event with us. Our planning committee wanted to do something special for you to show you just how thankful we are, so we created this luncheon as our way to say, 'thank you' to each and every one of you."

The room all joined together in applause as I had the entire the committee and catering staff to stand up. I waited for the room's applause to filter down before I spoke again.

"Now before we eat, my husband will say a blessing over the food." I handed the microphone to Randy and he proceeded to say grace over the food. After Randy said the blessing, we decided to walk around the room and formally introduce ourselves to our guests. The last person we met before we sat down was Xavier Latrell. It wasn't like we planned it that way, but due to him being fashionably late, we had to wait until he actually arrived at the church and got settled in.

As we walked over to the table where he was sitting, my heart began to palpitate faster than normal. It wasn't like I liked him or wanted to get with him or anything, but he was an extremely gorgeous man. He had smooth, caramel skin that appeared to be touched by the sun. The way he dressed commanded your very attention, and the scent of his cologne wafted through your nostrils until you had no choice but to take notice of him.

I hated to admit it but Xavier looked the same as he did on television and in magazines. He was absolutely flawless. He had beautiful white teeth, baby blue eyes, and an attitude that made you want to melt on the spot. I read in a few articles that his mother was African American and his dad was Caucasian which was the probably why he ended up with the bluest eyes I had ever seen on a person. Honestly, I didn't really care what the man was mixed with but the mere fact of the beautiful combination that was the only thing of importance to me. He was the type of man that made you wonder what type of woman generally caught his eye because he probably looked better than all of them put together.

Xavier wasn't the feminine looking type at all, but he was simply a beautiful man. If you weren't the one to fall in love with his looks then you were bound to fall in love with him after he opened up his mouth to sing. I was so glad that I walked over to him with my husband instead of walking alone. If I had to experience all of his fineness up in my personal space all at once alone, that would've been too much temptation for me. I definitely wasn't trying to appear as if I was some groupie. I was way classier than that.

From the moment we walked over to the area in which he was sitting, I couldn't stop smiling and I knew if I approached him initially I would come off as being overly anxious, so I was so relieved when Randy decided to speak first. I took a quick moment to compose my demeanor. I was determined to keep my cool at all cost.

"Hello, Mr. Latrell. I'm Pastor Randy Tate and this is my wife Denise. It's a pleasure to meet you and we appreciate you taking time out of your busy schedule to come here today." Randy stuck out his hand and Xavier extended his.

"The pleasure's all mine. I appreciate your ministry thinking of me and having me come. I count it such an honor to be here." He smiled and then he turned to address me.

"So nice to finally meet you. Welcome to Oakdale." I smiled and shook his hand.

"Thanks. I feel right at home here." Xavier replied, and then smiled back revealing a deep dimple in his left cheek. I began to pick up on the subtle way he was looking at me. It wasn't your regular type of glare, but it was the kind of stare that would have me completely naked if he could undress me with his eyes. It was something about the way he stared at me that had me uncomfortable, yet intrigued at the same time. I guess not having sex, gave me the ability to sniff those types of subtleties out like a hound dog.

Having Randy standing right next to me was surely a blessing in disguise, because everything within me wanted to be curious and probe into the very reason why he felt the need to stare so hard. I was a changed woman and definitely wasn't going to go down that road that easy. So I did the best thing I could do: I ignored his gestures all together.

Throughout the entire luncheon, I made it a point to casually glance over in Xavier's direction and sure enough he was already staring at me. I didn't pay any attention to the fact that he was staring. I acted as though I didn't see him at all. I was flattered and all, but he was mighty bold to be checking me out so blatantly when he knew my husband was sitting right next to me.

Toward the end of our gathering, I spotted Kenny walking through the hallways acting like he was working, when I knew good and well the fool wasn't doing anything. He looked over at me and I rolled my eyes and that didn't even faze him. He smiled and then gave me an air kiss. That fool really had no shame. I handed Kaylah to Randy and then I decided to go and use the restroom and freshen up a bit. I got up from the table, walked through the exit doors, and down the hall in the direction of where the restrooms were located.

HOLY REVENGE

I was so excited that the luncheon we'd planned for months was a complete success. I had a very good feeling that the entire conference would go just as we planned as well. After I washed my hands, and checked my appearance over in the mirror, I left the bathroom. I pushed the bathroom door open and bumped directly into someone.

"I'm so sorry. I didn't mean to bump into you." I said quickly, before I realized that I'd bumped into Xavier Latrell.

He held up his hand, placed it across his chest and flashed that dangerous smile of his.

"It's okay. You don't have anything to apologize for. I should actually be the one apologizing for not watching where I was going. So please forgive me." Xavier winked and then took my hand and planted a soft kiss on it. And then as quickly as he appeared, he disappeared down the hallway. I wonder if he did that on purpose.

As soon as I walked back into the luncheon, I was met at the door by public enemy number one...Daphne. She was waiting at the door for me like I had been gone an hour. Truth was I had only stepped out for five minutes. I silently prayed as I approached her, hoping that she would have something good to say instead of a complaint like she always did.

"Denise, this luncheon turned out to be very nice. I'm very pleased with how everything came together." Daphne smiled. I was slow in my response because I was waiting for her to follow up her compliment with a complaint, but the fact that she didn't have anything else to say really caught me off guard. I couldn't believe that she was actually paying me a compliment instead of hurling out insults and smart remarks.

"I'm glad you enjoyed yourself Daphne." I answered unsure of what else to say.

Jessica A. Robinson

"I know you're surprised that I'm giving you such nice remarks, but I believe in giving people their roses while they can still smell them."

I smiled. "Thanks."

Jesus must really be on his way back, because I never thought I'd see the day when Daphne had anything nice to say to me.

"Now, if we could only get you to start wearing 'holy attire' instead of skin tights, then we would be all the way good, but I guess you gotta crawl before you can walk." Daphne replied. She walked away leaving my mouth wide open. I walked back to the table where I was sitting and Mama Alice was holding Kaylah and talking to Randy.

"I saw Evilene over there talking to you. What in the world did she want?" Alice started to rock Kaylah, in her arms, as Kaylah giggled and laughed.

"She didn't want anything. She came over here to compliment me on how well the luncheon went and then she finished up her compliment with a smart remark." I chuckled. Alice began to shake her head back and forth.

"I pray every day that God touches my heart. I cannot stand that woman at all. Everything she does serves as a source of irritation for me." She closed her eyes and took a deep breath.

"I know Ma, me too. I have to ignore her most of the time" I agreed.

"I promise you if I didn't have the baby in my arms then I would be making a special trip over to where she is and slap Daphne upside her head. She better be glad I know the Lord." Alice huffed.

"Ma, please cut it out. Randy responded. I can't have you up in here trying to fight Daphne. She's not even worth your anger. You two know how she is, and even though you're fully aware, she still manages to get you worked up and she's just being herself."

"You're right about that son. She is not worth any of my energy or my time. I didn't even come over

HOLY REVENGE

here to talk about her. I was coming over to ask if you guys wanted me to keep Kaylah for you during the conference? Your father and I thought it might make it a little easier on you if we kept her."

My eyes lit up like a Christmas tree.

"For real? Mom you really don't have to. I know she can be a bit of a handful sometimes and if it's a problem I'll just have Marisol keep her during the day for us." I said as Alice turned her hand up at me.

"Don't be silly. You know we don't mind keeping our grandbaby, besides I raised Randy and Will and they were both two pieces of work, so keeping Kaylah is a piece of cake to me." Alice smiled.

"Thanks mom, I really appreciate you doing this, but you didn't have to put my business out there. I wasn't bad when I was little." Randy laughed.

"I don't know why you're in denial, but it's okay. You know you were bad...but anyway, you two don't worry about Kaylah. Take these few days without the baby to enjoy each other. I'll be by to get her in an hour or so." Alice replied before walking away.

Her last little statement before leaving left me sort of in a curious state. I wondered why she offered to keep the baby so that we could "enjoy" each other. Had Randy told her that we hadn't had sex in a long time or could she tell by our body language that there was some underlying problem going on? I didn't know exactly what it was, but I knew that Alice knew more than what she was willing to admit. And if my mother-in-law had been able to pick up on the fact that something was wrong, it made me wonder who else picked up on the same exact thing?

At this point I couldn't let my thoughts consume me. I didn't take a rocket scientist to figure out that Randy and I were legal roommates right now, and a blind person could see that absolutely nothing was going on in the bedroom. I knew one thing: I was going to take my mother-in-law's advice and enjoy my husband over the next few days. I know we haven't had sex, and he always tries to give me excuses, but I wasn't going to take 'no' for an answer this time. I was going to go home and set the mood so serious he wouldn't have a choice but to surrender to my plans. I was planning to put it on him so serious that he would never consider putting me on a sex strike ever again. Tonight would be the night where I would pull out all stops and leave him craving for more like he used to before Tyrone entered into the picture. I saw tonight as being my prime opportunity to make things happen and I wasn't going to back down until I got what I wanted.

After the luncheon, Randy and I went home and I started to pack Kaylah's things. Alice was such a punctual woman that I knew I better hurry up and get everything ready because she would be pulling up soon.

My house phone started to ring as I was helping Randy load the baby's things in his mother's car.

"Hey baby, let me go and grab that." I said, as I kissed Kaylah and ran in the house trying to catch the phone call before the person hung up.

"Hello sis! So you all finally made it back?" I said knowing it was my sister Michelle from the name on the caller I.D.

"Yes ma'am. We came back like an hour ago. I was calling to see if you were able to stop by. The boys really want to see you and I would like to kiss my baby Kaylah." Michelle said.

"Well, your baby just left with Mama Alice, but I'll still stop by and see my favorite lil guys. When do you want me to come?"

"You can come now if you want."

"Okay, I'll see you in a few."

I changed into a gray jumpsuit and took the short drive over to my sister's house on the west side. Randy decided to stay behind and get some rest. He was practically in a deep snore by the time I left the house. The July heat and sun beamed down on my car and made me break into a sweat as I drove, so I removed my jacket and tossed it in the back seat.

HOLY REVENGE

My phone began to vibrate several times and I picked it up only to find that I had a new text message. I grew irritated when I saw that it was from Kenny. I opened the message to reveal:

Hey Sexy,

I was so happy to see you today at church. I just wanted to rip your clothes off right then and there; but it wasn't the time or the place. But I know I'll have a chance sooner or later. I can't wait to taste you.

There was something about him that was so sexy, but at the same time he managed to get on my last good nerve. I stared at the message for a few minutes and instead of entertaining it, I ended up typing:

Kenny please stop texting me. If you text me something inappropriate like this again, I'll be forced to show your boss exactly what you sent to me.

Thanks and have a blessed day.

I smiled as I tucked my phone back inside my purse. I knew he wasn't expecting that text from me at all. I was safe to say that he probably wouldn't be texting me back for the rest of the day after that comment. I wish I could see the expression on his face. His mouth is probably hanging to the floor and I know he must be shocked to say the least. I guess it must suck to want something that you can't have.

When I pulled up in my sister's driveway, I saw my nephews, Junior and Jovan, playing in the front yard. They were throwing a football back and forth, but the minute I parked in the driveway they put it down and ran full speed to my car.

"Auntie Niecey! We missed you!" Junior screamed as he reached me first. I bent down and gave him a big kiss and then a hug. I used to be able to scoop him up in my arms, but at twelve he was almost as tall as me. I could probably still pick him up, but I would land myself in the hospital shortly after.

"I missed you too." I smiled.

"Where's Kaylah?" Jovan asked as he jumped into my arms and looked over my shoulder trying to see if she was in the car.

"She's with Grandma Alice." I answered as I kissed him one last time before putting him down.

"Aww man...I wanted to see her." Jovan replied.

"I know you want to see her. I'll bring her over so you two can play with her real soon. Where's your mommy?" I asked.

"She's in the house in the living room." Junior said, as they both ran back out in the yard and continued on with what they were doing.

I walked in the house and found my sister sitting on the couch removing things from their suitcases. She had such a tan that I would be surprised if she didn't have sunburn.

"Hey sis! So how was your vacation?" I asked as she got up from the couch and gave me a big hug.

"It was great. Jimmy, Me and the kids had such a wonderful time in Hawaii. I think we had more than just a good time, we barely wanted to leave."

"That's how vacation is supposed to be. I see you got a serious tan going on." I said pointing to the tan line on her arm.

"Yes I do. All I did was lay out on the beach, I swam, and sun bathed on the patio of our villa suite."

"Sounds nice, I've been to Hawaii once and I never stayed where you ended up staying. When Kaylah gets old enough to walk and enjoy a vacation like that we'll probably take her."

"Maybe we can all go together. Jimmy and I already decided that we're taking the kids next year. There was something for everyone to do. And I even did a little bit of shopping too." Michelle smiled. I loved seeing my sister in such a great mood. She had been through so much with her husband Jimmy; it felt so good to see them in such a good place.

Jimmy had went to counseling for alcohol and been clean for almost a year, been getting constant

HOLY REVENGE

promotions on his job, and attending church regularly. I must admit he had completely turned his life around. I was tired of seeing my sister depressed and crying all because he wouldn't act right, and I felt like she was too great of a woman to be dealing someone who brought her so much pain and grief.

"What in the world did you buy?" I asked.

"Speaking of shopping, I didn't just shop for me. I brought you something back too and for my baby Kaylah,"

"You didn't have to buy me anything sis, that's so nice of you," I smiled as she handed me two bags.

"Well, it's not much because I'm not rich like you and my brother-in-law, but there's a few things in there that I thought you would like."

I opened the first bag and saw a few picture frames that had the prettiest seashell design on them. Then I saw two T-shirts with 'Hawaii' written on them. And the last bag contained a few cute summer outfits for Kaylah.

I reached out and gave my sister a big hug.

"I love everything Michelle. You didn't have to get us anything at all. I'm glad you enjoyed yourself, that's enough for me."

"Girl please. All the times when I need you or need something you and Randy are always right there. I know I always say, 'thank you' but this time I wanted to get you a few gifts and say, 'thank you' again. Where is Randy?"

"He's at home—asleep."

"I understand because I feel myself about to go to sleep for the night as soon as Jimmy gets back from the store."

I picked up my keys and purse and stood to my feet.

"That's cool. Well, tell my brother-in-law that I said 'hello', and if you're not too busy this week, you know the conference starts tomorrow."

Jessica A. Robinson

"I'll be there. See ya tomorrow." Michelle said as she walked me outside and called the boys to come in the house because it was already getting dark outside. I couldn't believe that I had been over my sister's house for a few hours because it felt like more of twenty minutes, but time always has a way of flying when we're together. I kissed my nephews one more time and then got in my car and drove in the direction of my home. I was glad that I allowed Randy to sleep while I was gone because for what I had planned, he was going to need his full and complete strength.

I turned on my headlights and listened to Keyshia Cole's CD, *A Different Me,* while I drove. I noticed there was someone in a car behind me driving in the same direction I was going. I couldn't see who it was because they had tented windows, but I do know they followed me from the time I left Michelle's neighborhood and with each corner I turned, they turned too.

At first it didn't bother me because I realized there were more people than just me going in the same direction, but what disturbed me was the fact that they continued to follow me, even when I turned down streets that I knew would throw them off. I kept driving and listening to my music, hoping that they would get the hint and stop following me, but they not only continued to do so, but they even started to flash their lights at me.

My heart started to beat fast and it felt as though I was going to have a heart attack. I didn't want to call Randy and involve him in any of this mess, but I knew I really didn't have a choice at all. I pulled out my phone and began to call Randy when the mysterious car that I had never seen before sped around me and then disappeared in sight.

I didn't waste any time in driving directly home and praising God that whoever was following me got tired and decided to leave me alone. I pulled in my garage and immediately put the door down. I was so

HOLY REVENGE

relieved to be home. I was even happier to know that my husband was inside waiting for me. I wasn't planning on telling him I just got followed either. All that would do was kill the mood that I was about to create, and I wasn't going to let that happen at all.

When I walked in the house, I realized Randy was still in our bedroom. I thought he was asleep until I came in our master suite and saw him sitting on the couch in our sitting area watching some T.V.

"Hey baby, did you get some rest?" I asked as I walked over to him and gave him a kiss.

"Yes, I'm so glad I took that nap. Otherwise I probably would've been tired. How was Michelle and Jimmy's vacation?"

"Absolutely wonderful...she even brought us all gifts."

"That's nice."

"Baby, I'll be right back. I'm going to hop in the shower. I was outside with the boys and I smell like grass." I laughed.

"Ok babe. I'll be right here when you get out." Randy replied and laughed too. I walked over to my dresser and pulled out the new piece of lingerie that I brought a few months back. After I took a shower, I slipped on the black lace, V cut teddy with a matching robe that stopped in the middle of my thighs. I slipped on a pair of black, six inch heels, and applied some *Juicy Couture* perfume. I walked over to the full-length mirror that was in my bathroom and checked out my entire ensemble. I looked amazing to say the least. If he didn't have the desire to have sex with me before, then he would definitely feel the urge after he saw me in this outfit.

When I opened the bathroom door, Randy had kept his promise and was sitting in the same spot he was sitting in before I went in the bathroom. He was so engrossed in the television program he was watching that he hadn't even noticed that I'd come out of the bathroom. I didn't care in the least bit that he hadn't seen me, it gave me just enough time, and opportunity to do what I needed to do to set the stage for some romance. I waltzed over to our stereo system and put on Kem's *Intimacy* CD and then I dimmed the lights in our bedroom. I walked back over to where he was and joined him. My husband smiled as he checked out what I was wearing.

"Do you like what you see?" I asked, as I moved in closer to him, removed my robe, and then I proceeded to straddled him.

"Yeah, I like what I see. When did you buy this, it looks new." Randy said as he kissed me.

"I picked it up from *Saks* a couple of months ago. I thought it was only proper to break it out tonight." I wrapped my arms around his neck and began to kiss him hungrily. To my surprise he didn't hold back in his affection toward me. I felt relieved as his hands started to roam all over my body as if they were exploring unknown territory for the first time. I began to get chills up and down my spine at his touch. I removed his shirt and then started to unbutton his jeans. Almost instantly, things took an unexpected, yet familiar, turn.

"Stop." Randy said. I was still trying to kiss him when I thought I heard him say that, but I asked just to make sure I heard him clearly.

"What did you just say?" I asked.

"I said stop." He answered.

"Why, what's wrong *now*?" I turned my head to the side and raised my eyebrows in confusion.

"Nothing is wrong, we just need to stop."

"Well, obviously something has got to be wrong. What's the reason now Randy? You're tired or you have something else to do right now? I mean, I know you're a busy man, but you're not too busy to be with me and you can't even blame Kaylah because she's not even here!"

Randy shook his head 'no'.

HOLY REVENGE

"No, it's not that at all. I just don't want to tonight. I'm not really in the mood, okay?" Randy tried to feed me that excuse, but as far as I was concerned, I wasn't trying to hear that lame excuse. If anyone had a healthy appetite for sex it was surely Randy, and so for him to never be in the mood anymore was a lame excuse that I didn't believe. I wanted to hear the truth. I wanted him to give me the real reason as to why he didn't want to have sex with me anymore. I could smell a rat and I wasn't going to be satisfied until I got down to the actual truth.

"What do you mean, 'you're not in the mood?' You haven't been in the *mood* for a very long time. You barely want to touch me anymore, let alone have sex with me, so what's really going on?" I asked as I stared at him waiting for him to say something. I hoped he wouldn't give me another excuse like he'd previously been doing. He stared into my eyes and didn't say anything. Instead he looked down.

"Is there someone else?" I pressed my lips together and clenched my jaw as tight as I could. I knew I was being a bit precocious, but I felt the need to ask him that.

"Excuse me?" He lifted his head and looked at me. He looked at me like he couldn't believe what I'd just asked. I didn't budge or back down from what I just asked him. I crossed my arms and smacked my lips.

"You heard me. I wanna know if there is someone else? I mean come on, that has to be the only reason why our sex life is nonexistent. I know you Randy, and you have never gone this long without sex, so who are you sleeping with because it sure isn't me." I stated.

Randy laughed at my accusation as if I was telling a joke.

"You can't be serious Denise. I don't know why you've been so consumed with the fact that I'm cheating on you. You know I'm not sleeping with anyone, I would never cheat on you and you know that."

"Then what's going on?" I raised my voice. I waited and waited until finally Randy took a deep breath and answered me.

"Alright, look...I wasn't going to approach you with this, but the more and more I think about it, I definitely have to be honest with you and voice my concerns."

I nodded and didn't say anything. I let him continue to speak.

"It's not that I'm never in the mood or I'm messing around with someone else. I'm very much attracted to you baby, but sometimes I don't feel comfortable having sex with you and that's why I want you to go and get tested and then we can take it from there." He explained.

I raised my eyes and turned my head slightly as I tried to process what Randy just said.

"Wait a minute. So you're trying to tell me you want me to go and get tested before we have sex again? What you think, I have a disease or something? I had sex with one man, and you act like I had sex with fifty men." I got up from where I was sitting and put my robe back on. I went and planted my behind on the other end of the couch. I actually had sex with more men than I cared to count, but as far as my husband knew, Tyrone had been the *only* other man that I'd been with, and I planned on keeping it that way.

I knew that confession was good for the soul, and it was good to go to people and confess your sins, but those were the types of admissions I kept to myself. Besides, I had already prayed to God and asked for forgiveness, so why would I be required to tell Randy too?

When he found out about my affair with Tyrone, he'd asked me if there had been anyone else and I told him 'no'. Plain and simple. I knew it was wrong to lie to him, but if he really knew the complete truth about my sexual history, then he would automatically be done with me with no questions asked. Coming clean now would do nothing but piss him off even more, and I wasn't trying to do that.

"I understand that honey, but that one man could've had something serious that could potentially take one or both of our lives. I would rather we be safe, than sorry."

I laughed sarcastically at his little plea.

"I can't believe you right now. I really can't believe after all this time you want me to go and get tested. Why weren't you this insistent about it six months ago?"

"I know I may sound ridiculous to you right now, but just try and put yourself in my shoes right now. If I had been the one who stepped out on you and cheated, you'd probably be telling me the same exact thing."

"Huh, whatever. I would've never said that to you."

Randy threw up his hands at me.

"Okay I wasn't trying to get in a long debate with you over this. Either you want to be tested because I've asked you or not, it's very simple. But the final choice is up to you. I'm sleeping in my office tonight." Randy replied.

He then got up from the couch, walked out of our bedroom, and went downstairs. I couldn't believe what just happened. My husband had finally confessed to me the real reason why there wasn't any action going on between our sheets, and I was shocked.

He was the one who was so adamant about the whole 'forgiveness' thing and us moving forward in our marriage, and then he went and had to pull a stunt like this. If he was so concerned about his health, then why hadn't he demanded an STD test after Kaylah was born? I do remember telling him that I would do whatever it took to make our marriage work between us, but I couldn't help but feel that he may have went a little too far with his request on this one.

HOLY REVENGE

Chapter 9 (Randy)

I don't know why I'm so honest sometimes. Maybe if I learned to shut my mouth and answer things in a vague manner, then I could manage to keep the peace in my household. The person who ever said, 'honesty is the best policy' must've been drunk or smoking something; because look where honesty has gotten me. For the past five days, Denise and I haven't said two words to each other and I've been sleeping in my office since our fight. All because I came clean and was completely honest with her. Instead of things getting better with her, they seem to be getting worse.

I didn't really have too much time to dwell on my problems or to even talk about them because about twenty minutes ago my brother-in-law told me he was going to stop by the church and talk to me. A knock at my door interrupted my thoughts and I told him to come in.

"Hey Jimmy. What's up bro?" I asked as he took a seat across from me in my leather office chair.

"Nothing much. Just was coming by to check on you and see how you were doing. I haven't really seen you since Michelle and I come back from Hawaii."

"I know. Denise told me ya'll really enjoyed yourselves."

"We had a blast. We're planning on going back next year. Thanks for the recommendation and the help bro. We appreciate it." Jimmy smiled.

"No problem. I'm just glad I'm in a position to bless you, that's all." I leaned back in my chair.

"So how are you and Denise doing? How is everything on the home front Randy?" Jimmy asked. I knew by the nature of his question that he must've heard something from Michelle and since he was my brother-in-law it wasn't any need to lie about it.

"Denise and I had a fight almost a week ago, and she hasn't spoken to me ever since. She only speaks to me when we're here at church for the conference, but the minute we get in the car to go home she goes back in silence mode." I explained.

"Dang bro, what kind of fight did you two have that has her so quiet like that?" Jimmy asked.

"Well, she's quiet because she's mad at me obviously, but she's mad because I asked her to do something."

"And that is?"

"I asked her to go and get tested before we get intimate again. I know I'm kinda late, but I just didn't know how to ask her until now."

"Whoa, so that's what has Denise mad. I know your timing may be a little delayed bro, but it's not like you asked her to do something crazy. Truth be told, Michelle asked me to get tested when I cheated on her the last time, and even when my results came back and they were good, it still took me some time before that part of our marriage was restored."

"See, I thought having her go and get tested was the right thing to do. You see how many cases of people out here who catch all kinds of crazy diseases and they were devoted to their spouse. I don't want that to be me. I don't want that to be us. Denise is acting like I asked her to sell her body on the street."

"I'm not gonna lie. I was upset when Michelle asked me, but the more I thought about it, I felt that it was the least I could do considering all the hurt and pain I put her through. I snapped out of my selfishness after too long, believe me Denise will too."

"I sure hope so. Now she's acting like I'm air and I don't even exist, but that was after she asked me to come clean about not wanting to have sex with her. I don't understand bro, it feels like I'm being punished for being honest."

"I know what you mean. Don't back down though, stand your ground. I know she'll do what's right—if she wants to make your marriage work she will do whatever it takes."

"You're right. So enough about me, how have you been doing?"

"I've been doing great. I really like my new position at my job, its great money and I'm able to take care of my family the right way which is more important than anything. And as far as my drinking, I'm still clean and sober. I'm coming up on a year without touching any alcohol and I'm thankful to God because I never thought I would be able to say that."

"That's amazing. It's inspiring to watch you doing so good. I'm proud of you man." I replied.

"Thanks, I'm proud of me too. And I appreciate you sending me to that treatment facility in California. That really helped me to work through my issues."

"Don't mention it. I like to be able to bless those who are helping themselves. It's my pleasure."

Jimmy looked down at his watch and stood from his chair.

"I gotta run. I came over here to talk to you on my lunch break and now it's time for me to head back, but listen you don't worry about you and Denise, it's gonna all work out; trust me. I'll see you on Sunday morning." I walked around my desk and gave him a hug before he left my office.

I sat back down at my desk and stared at my computer screen. I know I was supposed to be working on my sermon for tomorrow's message, but my mind was the furthest thing from it. I tried to come up with more things to add to it, but for a half hour, all I could do was stare at the screen. With things being so crazy in my household, I couldn't seem to concentrate much. I minimized the *Word* document and put my computer in sleep mode. I got up and went to do the only thing I knew how to do in a time like this; I went to the sanctuary and prayed. I got on the altar, anointed

HOLY REVENGE

myself and prayed. I prayed for Denise, I prayed for me, I prayed for our family. I prayed for focus to complete what God was having me work on. I stayed there and I prayed until I felt the burden being lifted.

"Pastor, I'm so sorry to disturb you. I didn't mean to come in here and startle you like this." Myra said as she walked down the center aisle of the sanctuary just as I was finished praying.

"It's okay. You didn't disturb me. Is everything okay?"

"Yes, everything is fine."

"I'm surprised to see you here. I thought your plane was leaving today?" I asked.

"Well, it was supposed to leave, but I felt a heavy burden in my spirit to stay and the spirit of the Lord told me to come back here and pray."

"Wow. Well, feel free to pray for as long as you would like. And don't worry about your transportation, I'll have one of the ministers take you where you need to go."

"Thank you so much. Now, I don't know if you will agree with me or not, but I feel like God has given me a specific message for your church that I am to preach tomorrow, and if I'm allowed to, I would love to share it with your congregation."

I stood back for a few seconds with my arms crossed thinking about what she had just said.

"Okay Myra. That will be fine. I'll just save what I had previously prepared for another time. But like I said, please feel free to pray as long as you would like and I'll have one of the ministers take you back to your hotel and get you squared away. If you need me, I'm just a phone call away." I explained as I gave her a hug and then walked out of the sanctuary to find Kenny.

He was walking down the hallway to his desk when I caught up with him.

"Hey Kenny, I'm about to get out of here in a few minutes, but Myra Washington is still here. She's in the sanctuary praying and she'll be with us for one more day. She'll also be delivering tomorrow's message, so when she's done can you make sure our transportation department comes and takes care of her for one more night. She'll be staying at the same hotel and her flight will need to be changed as well." I said as Kenny scribbled notes down on a notebook that was sitting on his desk.

"No problem Pastor. I'll see to it that they do everything you've asked."

"See you later Kenny. And thanks again." I said, as I went to my office grabbed my keys and left the church. I glanced down at my watch and was thankful that Sunday service was taken care of so I didn't have to stare at that computer screen anymore. The sun was shining brightly and it was starting to get hot, but with the wind blowing, it created the most comfortable breeze.

I figured it would be a perfect day to go over to my parent's house and school my little brother, Will, on a few things concerning basketball. I know he may be a high school basketball star, but he couldn't see me at all on the court. I called his cell phone to make sure he was there and when I pulled up in the driveway he was waiting for me in his basketball gear.

"So, I see someone is ready to get beat down on the court today." Will said as he sat on the porch shooting the ball in the air practicing his shot. I swear my brother could be so cocky sometimes, but I couldn't say anything, because I was cocky at times too, especially when it had to do about something I was good at.

"I'm glad you're finally ready to take your beating like a man. Let me go and get changed, I'll be right back out." I laughed as I walked past him and into the house so I could change my clothes.

"Hey, mom, what ya doing?" I walked in and saw my mother sitting on the couch watching some soap opera.

HOLY REVENGE

"I'm good son, just catching up on my soaps. Your father is down the hall if you need him." She answered, apparently in her soap-induced trance. Seeing my mother so engrossed in her television show made me laugh.

"Okay, mom, I don't need dad. I'll go and speak with him, but I'm actually here to play Will in some basketball."

"Oh, okay, well, I'll come out and talk to you later, right now I'm trying to catch up." My mother replied. I gave her a quick kiss and then I went and changed my clothes. After I walked out of the bathroom, I went down the hall to my father's study to say, 'hello' to him, but when I saw he was asleep in his recliner, I turned back around and walked back outside.

"So, you ready for your beating boy?" I asked as I signaled for Will to pass me the ball. He smacked his lips and then passed it to me thinking I was going to drop it or not catch it, and I caught it with the precision of an *NBA* player.

"For a second there I thought you weren't going to come out. I thought Ma talked you into hanging up your jersey once and for all."

"Never that boy, never that. I'm too good to retire. If you knew what was good for you, you would step aside and take notes on my game 'cuz it's pure greatness."

"Please. The only thing great about your game is the fact that you can still walk at your age. But after today that's all gonna change. You might have to be wheeled in to the pulpit every Sunday messing around with me." Will boasted.

"Whatever; are you ready?" I asked him as I walked to our backyard where our basketball court was.

"I was born ready, let's go." Will said as he followed behind me and we proceeded to play basketball.

Jessica A. Robinson

An hour and a half and three games later, my brother was the victor and I was exhausted to say the least. I don't know if it was the heat beaming down on my head and my back that made me move slow, or it was the fact that I was just tired but my game sucked in a major way and I was almost embarrassed losing to my brother the way I did.

"Good game" My brother said as he drank an entire water bottle in one gulp. After he swallowed he looked at me and then burst out laughing.

"Go ahead and laugh, I know you were being sarcastic. My game sucked. Admit it." I said as I sat at the picnic table on the patio. He didn't waste any time in laughing at me.

"Bro, just admit it, you're getting old and I'm a fantastic player."

"You're right about one thing. I may be getting old." I laughed and then continued. "You are a great player Will. And your game has gotten so much tighter since the last time we played. You're really serious about this aren't you?"

"I'm trying to be. Well, as much as dad will let me be." Will said.

"What's that supposed to mean?"

"You know how dad is, if I'm not talking about going to seminary school, then he doesn't want to hear anything about it."

"That's what he said?"

"Basically, in so many words. I told him that I really want to try and take a stab at trying to play ball in college and go to the *NBA* and he doesn't even want to talk about it. And I have a good chance too. I'm not even in my senior year yet and college scouts are already calling the high school asking about me. All kinds of schools, *Big Ten* schools and every other school you can imagine."

"Does Mom and Dad know about all this?"

"They do and when I tried to bring it up to dad, he didn't want to even talk it over with me. He said God

HOLY REVENGE

told him that both of his sons would be in ministry and be preachers just like him. I'm not doubting God or anything, but I just don't believe I'm supposed to be a preacher bro."

"I totally understand where you're coming from. There was a point and time where I wanted to go to college and become a lawyer, and who knows, maybe one day I might get the urgency from the Lord to go and pursue that, but I'm a Pastor because that's what God has called me to do, and I feel you should pursue what God is calling you to do."

"See, why doesn't Dad see things the way you do? We've been going back and forth about this for the past few months and he isn't seeming to budge at all. I really feel like God has given me this talent. I'm not trying to turn my back on God at all, I just want to pursue what I love to do and that's basketball for me. It's all I do, all I think about."

"I agree with you and here's what I'll do. I'll go and talk to Dad for you, and try to get everything worked out for you; how does that sound?" I asked.

He grinned and nodded.

"That sounds good. If he'll listen to anybody, I know he'll listen to you. You always seem to get him to see everything from both sides."

"No problem bro, all I need you to promise me is that you'll send me free tickets to all your games. I want to be right there cheering you on."

"Count it done." My brother said, as he slapped hands with me and we went inside to cool off. I decided to take a shower at my mother's house instead of taking one at home since I was already there and once I stepped out of the shower, I had a text message from Alexis on my phone:

*Hey Junior...I see you're next door at
your parent's house. Would you mind
stopping by before you leave. I would
like to talk to you.*

I deleted the message and then finished getting dressed. After I tied my *Air Force One's,* I talked to my parents for a few minutes and then walked across the yard until I made it to the front door. I knocked a few times and then I heard Alexis scream that it was open, so I let myself in and sat in the living room in the same spot I was in the last time I was there. I wondered what she wanted to talk to me about. Whatever it was I hoped that it was quick and straight to the point, because I really wasn't in the mood to get into another altercation with a woman. My argument with Denise was enough.

"Hey, Junior, I'm so glad that you can come over. I was just getting ready to text you when I saw you out back trying to keep up with your little brother," She snickered.

"Trying to keep up? I was keeping up...matter of fact, Will was trying his hardest to keep up with me." I boasted. All Alexis did was laugh.

"Oh really. It looks like he was giving you a run for your money." She laughed.

I tried to remain prideful, but Alexis could see straight through me. In all honesty, Will whooped my behind in basketball. My brother was that good. I started laughing right along with Alexis.

"Yeah, you're right. He kicked my butt to say the least. I can't wait to see him play college ball. But enough about me, I came over because you said you wanted to talk."

"Yeah, I did—I do want to talk to you. Hold on one second, I'll be right back." Alexis said, as she disappeared down the hallway. She came back with two glasses of sweet tea.

"Thank you." I said as she handed me the glass.

"So, what's on your mind Alexis?' I said taking a long sip of my drink.

"I've been doing a lot of thinking and I feel like it was time that you and I have a talk."

"About..."

HOLY REVENGE

"The way I left fifteen years ago. I've really been thinking about it, and I want to apologize. I shouldn't have left here the way I did, and most of all I shouldn't have left you." She said as she took a deep breath and exhaled. So she finally admitted she made a mistake when she left me all those years ago. I remember how I used to always envision this day, and how I would respond when she actually had the nerve to admit she was wrong, and all the things I was going to say to her, but remarkably I felt none of those things.

"That's why you called me over here to apologize about what happened over fifteen years ago? You didn't have to do that. I've moved on and I know you've moved on, so an apology is not necessary." I said as I smiled trying to lighten the load. Truth was I really didn't want to go there with her, so brushing off the entire conversation was going to help me from really travelling back all those years ago.

"No, Randy, I needed to apologize. I had no business from running away from the only person that has ever loved me for real. I didn't know true love until you, and I've never experienced it since. I didn't realize how much you meant to me until I had already left, and I was so stupid for letting you get away. It's something I think about every day. We should be together. That should be me helping you run the ministry and having your children, that should be me and no one else, and I don't know how I will ever forgive myself." Alexis said as she began to cry.

"I know you feel like that should be you instead of my current wife, but the reality of it all Alexis is you are the one that left. You're the one who walked away from me when all I wanted to do was spend my life making you happy. And since you did walk away from everything, including me, then it just wasn't God's will for us to be together, and I'm okay with that. I understand how you feel you made a mistake, but that's something we all do and it just wasn't meant to be."

"So, that's all you're gonna say, that we weren't *meant to be,* but I know the same way I felt about you is the same way you felt about me. Why won't you just admit it?" She asked as I began to feel myself getting mad.

"See that's just like you Alexis, selfish...only thinking about yourself and hear what you wanna hear. Well, I'm sorry, the world doesn't work that way. It never has and it never will." I tried to convince Alexis with what I was saying, but I didn't even really believe all that myself.

"I admit, I've been selfish in the past, but I'm not afraid to admit it. You're gonna honestly sit here and tell me you don't feel anything for me at all? So this is just all me huh?" She asked and before I could even bring my case up against her in protest, she leaned in and kissed me with a force that made me feel like I had got hit in the face with a fifty pound brick. She had managed to kiss me so fast that I was caught off guard. I tried to remove my lips from the kiss, but for some reason they were stuck and remained locked in position with hers. Finally I got some strength from somewhere and was able to pull away.

"I'm so sorry." Alexis said as she looked at me and put her head down. I guess that was really my cue to leave and I was definitely taking the way of escape that God had provided for me, before I did anything else. I stood and Alexis got up from her seat too.

"It's okay. No need to feel sorry. It was an accident. I have to go, so I'm gonna just...yeah..." I replied as I started walking toward the front door without even looking back at all.

"Goodbye Alexis." I said as I turned the knob for the door and left her house as fast as I could.

I really couldn't even be mad at Alexis. I know she just admitted to me that she still had feelings for me, and how marrying my wife was a mistake since she felt like that was supposed to be her, and she even hauled off and kissed me, but it wasn't like I pulled

HOLY REVENGE

away or tried to stop her. The way I see it, I was just as guilty as her. I could see that time really hadn't changed anything with Alexis. She had always been a little selfish when it came to the things she wanted in life. Thinking that the entire world was spinning on an axis that only she had control of, but it doesn't.

She tried to pull me into her way of thinking like she always did back in the day, and I wasn't even trying to fall for it, but the problem was, at this very moment, she had my nose wide open and if I didn't go home and pray about this situation quickly I might not have the strength to resist her any longer.

"Denise." I called out her name just as I walked into my office after Sunday morning service. She didn't answer me at all. She pretended to be preoccupied and searching through her purse when she knew good and well that I was calling her. I knew she wasn't looking for anything in that overpriced purse anyway.

"Baby did you hear me?" I asked and looked over at her. She still seemed to be caught up with whatever was in that *Coach* purse of hers. She finally sighed and then put her purse down beside her.

"Did you want me?" She asked as she rolled her eyes and then smiled. I hated when she was sarcastic.

"Yeah, baby, I've only been calling you for the past few minutes. You act like you didn't hear me. What's up?"

"Nothing's up, why?" She asked.

I shook my head and studied her facial expression. I knew she was still upset about what I had asked her to do. I could tell by the way her nostrils flared and how her lips had a slight twist in them that she still had an attitude.

"Come on, something is wrong. You haven't really said anything since the other day."

"I promise you I'm fine. The reason why I haven't said anything lately is because I really have nothing to say."

"Are you still mad about what I asked you to do?" I asked and before she graced me with an answer, there was a knock at the door.

"Myra, you did such a wonderful job speaking this morning." Denise changed the subject as soon as she seen Myra and one of our associate ministers escorting her into my office.

"Thank you so much Denise. I knew it was meant for me to stay and deliver this Word today. I'm just thankful for you and your husband for allowing me the freedom to do so." Myra said as I motioned for her to take a seat in one of my leather chairs.

"Oh, don't thank me, thank my husband. He's always making decisions straight from the Lord. When the Lord says move and do something, he always does without a second thought; isn't that right honey?" Denise said, as she gave me a big smile which I knew was faker than patent leather. She was trying to be smart on the sly, I knew exactly what she was doing. She was referring to the fact that I allowed Myra to stay and preach on Sunday without discussing it with her first. That was probably another reason why she wasn't speaking to me today. I wasn't under the impression that I had to consult her on every *little* thing concerning the ministry. Besides, she never got mad when we had other male speakers take my place at the last minute if they were in town. I think she was just bothered in the fact that Myra was a woman, and a good looking woman at that, stealing her shine for the week she was here.

"Myra it was meant for you to be here and share the Word with Oakdale this morning. My wife and I praise God for you" I answered and looked over at my wife who was trying her best to hold herself together, even though I know she practically wanted to rip my head off.

"Thank you so much Pastor. I really appreciate that."

HOLY REVENGE

"Don't mention it. I like to call you a secret weapon. When people first meet you, they see a pretty face and think you're all smiles, but when you open up your mouth to deliver the Word of God, you come with the precision of a two-edge sword. I'll tell ya one thing; I definitely didn't see that coming." I explained. Myra smiled and Denise rolled her eyes. I knew she was irritated by my last statement, but I didn't care. I knew she felt threatened by Myra's presence, but she had nothing to worry about as far as I was concerned.

"So when does your flight leave Myra?" Denise asked as she tried to break up the praise fest that was taking place.

"My flight leaves in three hours. I have to speak at another conference in Philly tonight and tomorrow morning." She answered and Denise looked down at her watch and then focused her attention back on Myra.

"Well, we'll get transportation to drive you straight to the airport. We wouldn't want you to miss your flight."

"That's very nice of you. I would like that." Myra replied.

"Good, let me excuse myself. I'll go and get one of our drivers and they will see to it that you get there and on time." Denise got up from where she was sitting and left out of my office. I had to chuckle slightly at my wife who was trying to appear all helpful, but was the furthest thing from help itself. She was so funny sometimes, especially when she was upset about something. It took her less than five minutes to come back and send Myra on her way.

"Well, it was such a pleasure to come to your ministry. I've really enjoyed myself and I pray that God's favor and blessings rest on your ministry. This isn't the last you'll be seeing of me." Myra gave Denise and me a big hug.

"Let's definitely keep in touch. God Bless you." I replied as everyone left except for me and Denise. I wanted to resume our conversation from where we were before everyone walked in, but my cell phone began to buzz on top of my desk and I went around and picked it up.

Junior,

I'm so very sorry about what happened between us yesterday. It was a mistake and I apologize from the bottom of my heart. Hope you can forgive me.

Alexis

I replied:

All is forgiven Alexis, and I forgive you. Yes, it definitely was a mistake and cannot happen again. Take care.

Randy

I deleted both of the messages and then placed my phone back down. When I looked at Denise, I could tell by the look on her face that she was curious as to who had just sent me a message.

"Who was that?" She asked.

"Oh, someone sent me an email and I was just responding to them." I answered quickly.

"Yeah, whatever." Denise replied and then picked up her car keys.

"Well, I'm about to go home because I'm tired. Are you coming now too?"

"I'll be coming home in a little while. I have a few things to finish up here before I leave." I said as I walked her to the door. Before she walked out and left without saying anything, I grabbed her and pulled her in close to me.

"Baby, I hate it when we're mad at each other like this. We'll work everything out."

"Yeah okay." Denise sighed and then left my office.

I knew Denise was still mad about me asking her to get tested but those were one of the things that she was going to have to do. I wasn't going to

HOLY REVENGE

compromise in that area at all. I'd rather be safe than sorry.

Chapter 10 (Terri)

"So, why don't you want to be tested again?" I asked Denise as we were walking down an aisle in the grocery store. You would've thought I just asked my best friend something really crazy by the way she was looking at me. Before she even answered my question, she put her finger up to her mouth telling me to be quiet. Then she began looking around the grocery store trying to see if someone was paying attention to our conversation, which I could clearly see they weren't.

"Girl, I'm sorry. I didn't mean to do that to you, but you just never know who's listening and I definitely don't need anyone else up in my business."

"I understand, but what's your issue with being tested for STD's? It's so important to be tested nowadays, especially since African-American women are among the leading group of women being infected with HIV. I'd rather you be safe than sorry." I made sure I lowered my voice to almost a whisper.

"That's understandable, but the issue I have with him is how he had the nerve to ask after all this time, like I'm dirty or something. I'm embarrassed that he would even demand this of me. I would never ask him to do this if he was in my position" Denise said as she crossed her arms and looked at me trying to convince me that her last statement was true, and I wasn't buying what she just said at all.

"Now you know that's a lie straight from the pits of hell. If Randy cheated on you, you would've reacted the same way he did, if not worse. You forget that I know you like the back of my hand." I looked back at her and although she tried to hold in her laugh she couldn't. We both started laughing. She definitely couldn't fool me.

"Quit trying to make me laugh Terri. I know it may sound funny, but this is serious. You do have a point, but I'm saying I messed around with one man and he acts as though I messed around with the whole entire city."

"Newsflash, you've messed around with more than just one man and let's not even take into account all the women these men have slept with in addition to you. So being tested is the best thing I feel you should do, and if that's what's going to make your husband happy I say do it."

"I know, he just made me upset when he sprung that on me the other day."

"Well, if it makes you feel any better, Carlos and I both went and got tested before we did anything."

"And that's understandable for you two because you aren't married, but this is my husband we're talking about, but I guess you don't see things my way because you're on team Randy." Denise smacked her lips.

"Don't be silly, I can see where you both are coming from. If I were you, I would do what he's asking. You have to meet him in the middle on this one. Isn't that what marriage is all about?" I asked as she smiled.

Even though she probably wouldn't admit, Denise knew what I was telling her was right.

"You're right. Even though being tested is the last thing I want to do, I'll do it if that's what's gonna end my severe bedroom drought."

"I know you're making the right decision." I answered.

"So are you excited about dinner tonight?" Denise asked as she started picking up a few items off of the shelf and putting in the shopping cart.

Jessica A. Robinson

"Of course I'm excited and I'm nervous too. I wish you would let me come over early and help get everything ready for the dinner party."

"What are you nervous about? There's nothing to be nervous about. We're going to all get together and have a great time. And don't you worry about trying to help me do anything for dinner. I'll pull everything together. You just make sure you look fabulous tonight."

"Oh, I plan on it." I smiled. "I don't doubt that we're gonna have a great time but you know how my parents can be, that's why I'm nervous." I admitted. My parents always made me nervous when it was time for them to meet the man I was dating. It was something about my father's interrogation and my mother's sickening sweetness that was a dangerous combination and I hoped and prayed that they were on their best behavior tonight.

"Your parents will be fine. Don't worry. Randy and I will be there anyway to throw interference if things get too intense. No worries."

"You're right." I answered hoping to believe those very words.

After Denise and I left the grocery store, I went to my stylist Maurice Gooch and got my hair done and then I went home and took a long, relaxing bath. Carlos and I were going to ride together until he told me he had some business to finish up at work and he'll just meet me there. That didn't bother me anyway because I wanted what I was wearing to be a surprise for tonight.

I stretched across my bed and decided to catch up on a few episodes of my favorite show, *Hoarders,* when my house phone rang. The number flashing across the screen wasn't a familiar one to me, but I decided to answer the call anyway.

"Hello." I said as I sat up on my bed.

"Is this Terri?" The woman on the other line asked.

"Yes, this is Terri, why who is this?" I inquired.

HOLY REVENGE

"Well, that's really not important at this point. I'm just calling to warn you about a certain someone in your life. If you think Carlos is the one for you and he's a perfect little angel, well guess again. He's far from that and if I were you, I would be careful unless you wanna end up like I did. Watch your back girl; he's not the person he portrays himself to be." The woman said, and before I could say anything else to her, she hung up the phone.

I tried redialing the same phone number that had previously called me and all it did was ring. No one answered the line. I found that odd because I had never had anyone that I didn't know just call me out the blue like that, and then on top of that, they want to call and warn me about my man? I started to get upset, but after a few minutes I was able to calm myself down because in all the time I had known Carlos, he had never changed.

He was the sweetest, most honest person I had ever met and he had never given me a reason to think otherwise. It probably was one of his jealous ex-girlfriends that didn't want to let him go now that he had really found someone that he truly cared about. That's how things always went. You don't realize what you have until it's gone, and that woman on the other line was probably regretting the fact that she ever let Carlos go. Well, her loss was my gain, and her trash is definitely my treasure. I wasn't going to let that stupid phone call ruin my evening and I definitely wasn't going to let it bother me at all.

"How do I look?" I said as I waltzed into my best friend's house wearing a royal blue, *Herve Leger* dress. I spun around so she could check out my appearance. A huge smile crept across her face.

"Honestly, you look like a million bucks." she replied.

I took a deep breath and exhaled.

Jessica A. Robinson

"I know I'm tripping, but you know wearing a dress like this is new for me. I would much rather wear a pantsuit, but I'm trying to switch things up a bit."

"Well, you look gorgeous to say the least, and you have the right shape to wear a dress like this."

"Thanks Denise. Am I showing too much?" I asked as I looked at myself in the huge floor to ceiling mirror that was in the foyer.

"Absolutely not. You look fine. So where's the mystery man? I can't wait to meet him."

"He's on his way. He had a few things to finish up at work. He said he'll be on his way shortly. I hope that's okay."

"Yes, this is your evening honey. Whenever he comes will be just fine."

"Oh, and Bonnie and Clyde the church edition, will be here any minute now too." I laughed.

"You are wrong for that. Follow me; I want to show you all the food that I cooked." Denise snickered.

Denise took me by the hand and walked down the hall to their private dining room where she had everything arranged perfectly on the table.

"You did all of this for me?" I asked as I looked at all the food.

"I sure did. I wanted this evening to be special for you. I mean after all, you never know this Carlos guy may be the one for you." Denise replied and I smiled like I always did when I heard his name.

"There's a huge possibility that he might be." I answered. I got the sudden urge to open up to Denise and tell her about the anonymous phone call that I received earlier that day, but I kept that to myself. I didn't want anything to interfere with tonight. We were interrupted by the doorbell ringing and before we made it to the door Randy came down the steps to open it.

"Hey, Theresa and Eddie it's so good to see you." Randy said as he hugged both of my parents.

HOLY REVENGE

"It's so good to see you too." Theresa said as she kissed him on the cheek. My mother then walked over to me and Denise.

"Baby, you look wonderful. So where's Mr. Carlos? Your father and I can't wait to meet him."

"He's not here yet, but he should be here soon."

"Okay, that's fine."

"I'll be right back, I think I left Kaylah's pacifier in the kitchen and I can hear her starting to fuss. Excuse me for one moment." Denise announced and I was right on her heels.

"Well, I'll come with you. I wanna give my god daughter a kiss." I smiled.

We went upstairs to the nursery and found Kaylah struggling to stay asleep. She was holding the little brown teddy bear I brought her, and whining but the minute Denise gave her the pacifier, she was out like a light again. I bent over the crib and gave her a quick kiss.

"I miss her so much; I'm coming to get her at some point this week."

"You know that's fine with me. You can take her anytime."

The doorbell rang again and I turned to Denise and smiled.

"It's showtime Denise."

"Sounds like it is."

"Let's get downstairs before my parents eat him alive."

By the time we made it downstairs, Carlos was already in the house being greeted my Randy and my parents.

"Carlos this is my best friend and dinner our host Denise." I introduced them. Carlos stuck out his hand to shake hers, but Denise held her arms out instead.

"I give hugs Carlos; I'm sorry." She smiled.

"It's fine. I like hugs." He smiled back.

Jessica A. Robinson

"Well, since everyone is here, let's all go to the dining room where dinner will be served."

We all made our way into the dining room and took a seat at their long table and before we got the okay to eat Randy stood up and blessed the food.

Father God we just wanna say, 'thank you' for this time of fellowship. I pray a special blessing over the food that it will be nourishment to our bodies, in Jesus name, Amen.

"The dinner I've prepared is very casual, and since it is buffet style everyone can serve themselves. I hope you enjoy." Denise said as my parents got up and were the first ones to make themselves a plate.

"Don't worry about getting up, I'll fix your plate for you." I said to Carlos. I thought I had said it in a low enough voice where no one else heard me, but I threw that idea out the window once I saw my best friend wink at me on the sly.

I smiled and got up from my seat and fixed his plate and then I went back up to fix myself a plate. I know I shocked a lot of people when they observed me waiting on Carlos hand and foot, but I didn't care. He was a good man, and I wanted him to know that I could take care of whatever he needed. In the past, I never was this attentive toward my man and his needs, but times were changing for me.

"Randy and Denise I want to thank you for inviting me to dinner at your house. This food is really good and your house is absolutely beautiful." Carlos said in between bites. He loved to eat.

"It's our pleasure, and thank you for coming, we appreciate it. We're just glad we finally got to meet you." Randy replied. My dad finished chewing up the food he had in his mouth and wiped the remnants off of his face with his dinner napkin. I knew that meant only one thing: he was ready to start his questioning. I started praying hard because either this night was going to be a complete success or an absolute disaster.

HOLY REVENGE

"So Carlos, my daughter tells me that you're an architect?" He asked. I don't know why he was trying to act all absent minded now when every time he saw me he asked me what Carlos did for a living.

"Yes, sir. Actually, I'm an architect and I'm originally from Texas, but my company that I own, has several projects that we're working on here in the city." He explained.

"Okay, that's a good thing. So that means you have money coming in. I can't be mad at that." I smiled at my father's comment and then at Carlos who smiled back at me.

"So you're from Texas huh? Does your family live there too and your kids?" My dad asked. My eyes got big like they were about to pop. I honestly wished he would go back to enjoying his food rather than play twenty-one questions with my man.

"Yes, my entire family lives in Texas, and no I don't have any kids." Carlos chuckled.

"Okay, so you're a single man who makes good money, and has no kids...are you psycho or something? What's wrong with you?" Eddie inquired. I shook my head and playfully said, "Daddy."

"What baby?" He asked as if he didn't have a clue as to why I was calling his name.

"Why don't you eat the rest of your food, it's getting cold." I suggested. Since he wanted to play the clueless role, I was going to try my best and derail him from his current focus.

"I'll eat my food, don't worry. But Carlos and I are having a good conversation right now." My dad said then turned his attention back to Carlos and folded his hands on top of the table in front of him.

"Go ahead, I'm listening." He said as he gave Carlos the cue to speak.

"With all due respect sir, I'm not psycho. I'm not crazy at all. Just haven't found the right woman. I've dated around and all of the women I've come into contact have been wrong for me, but ever since I've met

Terri she's changed all that." Carlos took me by the hand before he continued.

"She's changed the way I view women and I'm so glad she's in my life." I winked at Carlos. It was like he always knew the right things to say.

"Well, you seem to be the man with all the answers and good ones I might add. Let me leave you alone before you accuse me of picking on you."

"It's perfectly fine, you can ask me whatever you want and I'll answer it to the best of my ability." He replied and then kissed me on my cheek.

"I like him." My mother said as she gave me the thumbs up. She didn't surprise me at all. I knew she was in the love the minute Carlos opened his mouth. It didn't take much for her to fall in love with a person. She had such a loving and caring spirit that there weren't too many people that she didn't like, and if she didn't particularly care for you, you knew it.

"I like him too, but let's see how I feel about him at the end of the night." My dad smiled and then continued eating his food. I was so happy that Carlos had made such a good impression on my parents, as well as my friends. He exhibited so much confidence and composure and wasn't easily intimidated by my father.

With me being such a pit bull in the courtroom, it felt good to have an equally as dominant man by my side. I had finally met my match. I loved the fact that he wasn't afraid of anything or anyone. He had the type of take charge attitude that could keep me grounded. Even though he exuded so much strength, there was still a sudden smoothness about him that alluded to the fact that he was not only book smart, but also street smart as well, and to me that was the perfect combination.

At the end of the evening, my mother was still in love with him, and my father and Carlos were making plans to go golfing in the near future, so I knew he definitely had won them over. We walked my

HOLY REVENGE

parent's outside and then went back inside to finish up our conversation with Randy and Denise.

Randy and Carlos walked down the hall to his study. They said they were going to watch a little *ESPN* while Denise and I went upstairs to her bedroom. She said she wanted to talk to me and I was dying to know what she thought of my man. I walked in behind Denise and she closed her bedroom door behind me.

"Girl, they keep playing on my phone." Denise said as she sat down on her bed and removed her heels.

"Who's playing on your phone?" I asked.

"I honestly don't know Terri, but whoever it is they won't stop calling me. They call my cell phone all day, every day, and instead of things getting better they are getting worse. Every time I dial the number back it doesn't go through. And get this, the other day someone followed me home from my sister's house."

"So have you told Randy any of this?" I took her shoes and put them on the shelf in her walk-in closet.

"I haven't told him anything. We're barely even speaking to each other as it is, and me mentioning anything about some anonymous callers will only add stress to the situation."

"Denise, I don't know about you keeping this from Randy. I think he has a right to know what's going on so he can be aware of it."

"I know I should tell him, and I do plan on telling him, just not right now. Besides I'm just thankful these fools haven't started calling the house yet and the person that was following me actually turned off onto another road after a while."

"Please don't hold this from Randy. He needs to know."

"I'll tell him. I promise." Denise replied and then she quickly changed the subject.

"So it's so nice that we finally got to meet Carlos. He is really good man. I like him for you." She smiled, which caused me to have a *Kool-Aid* smile once again.

"You like him for me for real?" I asked as I plopped down on her bed and we discussed him like we were a bunch of sixteen year olds.

"Yes, for once I feel like you've finally met someone that fits you in all sense of the word. He's successful, making his own money, he's drop dead gorgeous, and doesn't have any baggage. He also isn't intimidated by your strength, and I think that's an important quality to find in a man. You're a very successful woman who has done great things, and every man can't handle that. I really do think he's the one for you."

"Me too, I can really see myself with him in the long run. But I do need your opinion on something."

"What's up?" Denise asked me.

"Well, I got a phone call earlier today and it was from a woman whom I guess used to be with Carlos and she was telling me that I need to be careful because he is not who he claims to be and he'll break my heart. What do you think about that?" I was eager to hear my best friend's outlook on the whole situation. She always had a way at looking at things differently.

"I honestly don't think you need to focus on what some anonymous person has to say about your man. Do you even know this lady at all?"

"Not at all."

"Nope. She didn't even tell me who she was."

"Sounds like a hater if you ask me. She probably knows that he has finally moved on and is happy with you and she's bitter about it. That's all to it."

"So, I shouldn't worry about him?"

"Has he ever given you a reason to think otherwise about him?"

I shook my head, 'no'.

"Well, just chalk it up to the fact that someone is hatin' on your relationship, and don't even focus on that phone call anymore. Whoever called you is just mad because they can't have him. Just ignore people like her." Denise replied.

HOLY REVENGE

I wish it was that easy to just ignore someone and even though I tried to push all the thoughts about that phone call out of my mind, I couldn't stop thinking about it. I also couldn't stop thinking that the anonymous caller on the other end of the line was none other than Estella.

Chapter 11 (Denise)

"Yes, Jackson, that's my spot daddy! Right there!" I screamed as loud as I possibly could. I knew I should've been trying to be as quiet as I could, taken the fact that I was having sex with another man that wasn't my husband, but at that moment I really didn't care. It felt good to be in the arms of my former lover who knew exactly where my G-spot was.

It wasn't like I planned to fall into temptation, but it happened merely by accident and mere coincidence. It all started this morning. I went to the church and did a few things that needed to be done and then kissed my husband goodbye. I drove to the Mercedes Benz dealership on Mahoning Avenue and figured I would get my car serviced and have them fix my disc changer as well. There were so many people in the waiting room that I found the only unoccupied seat in the entire room and sat in it.

I had to sit next to a man that was snoring loud like a grizzly bear and a woman who had three kids running wildly around the waiting area. I was annoyed to say the least, but I tried my best to tune them out. Thank God I had brought my *iPod* along with me; otherwise I would've been miserable. I was so engrossed in trying to find a certain song that I didn't even see Jackson walking over to me until he was right in front of my face. He was waving his hands in front of my face trying to compete with my loud music. Once I looked up and saw him standing there, I removed my earphones and put it back in my purse.

"Oh my God Jackson, what are you doing here?"

"Obviously getting my Mercedes fixed just like you are. I'm surprised to see you here." He smiled as I stood up and gave him a hug. I was immediately hit by the expensive cologne that had become one of Jackson's trademarks. That man smelled so good. I knew I should've just hugged him quickly and let him go, but I stayed in his embrace for a few seconds longer and let the intoxicating smell linger in my nostrils.

He had to be one of the best smelling, best looking, best dressed men I knew. Age didn't do anything for him but cause him to look better and better. He was like that age old wine that got better and better with time.

"I'm surprised to see you also. It's been a while since we saw each other."

"It has been a long while hasn't it? Actually the dealership is pulling my rental car around front because my car won't be fixed until tomorrow. Why don't you join me?" Jackson asked.

I glanced down at my watch and then pondered on his offer for a moment. There was a part of me that knew that I shouldn't go anywhere with Jackson at all because he was too much of a temptation for me and that would be like setting myself up for a fall indefinitely, but there was another part of me that felt like going out with him would be harmless. It would be the equivalent of two old friends catching up. Nothing more and nothing less. Besides, he was giving me an opportunity to leave with him so I wouldn't have to be stuck in that overcrowded, noisy room. The latter of my initial thoughts won, and before I knew it I was walking out with Jackson and leaving the dealership. I felt like I could control myself and handle things if they got out of hand. It wasn't like I wanted to have sex with him anyway.

Not too many words were exchanged between us. I took turns glancing out the window and then over at Jackson who still had it going on. Time had definitely been on his side and the salt and pepper hair that he was sporting made him even sexier than before. I normally wasn't attracted to older men, but it was something about Jackson that made him irresistible and made me forget how old he was. The man knew how to look at you and make all of your rational thoughts disappear. Jackson pulled up to the *Residence Inn* and parked his car very close to the entrance of the building.

I didn't think we were going to go to his hotel. I had assumed that we were going to go to a restaurant and catch up over lunch. I really couldn't be all that shocked because when we were together that's usually the first place we went. I decided I was going to keep my cool at all cost. I didn't want him picking up on the fact that I was nervous. We were in fact old friends.

"So how long have you been in town?" I asked as I got out of the car and did a quick scan of the parking lot to see if I recognized any one or the cars. I breathed a sigh of relief as there were only a few cars in the entire lot. I was actually glad he parked so close to the front door because we were able to slip in the building without bringing any attention to ourselves. The teal stilettos I wore with my skinny jeans sounded like two-hundred pound boulders as they met with the marble floor. The sound they made would've caught someone's attention if they were in the lobby. So when I saw that the entire lobby was empty including the front desk, I was relieved. The last thing I needed was to run into someone that I knew when I was up in this hotel with Jackson. We walked over to the elevator and took it up to the fourth floor where his suite was. He slid the key in its slot, and then opened the door to reveal a beautiful hotel room.

"This is very nice; I didn't even know they had rooms to look like this."

"Yeah, they're one of my favorite hotels to stay in no matter where I am in the world." He grabbed the door handle and shut it behind him. I walked down the steps into the living room and took a seat on the couch.

HOLY REVENGE

Before he joined me, he took off his suit jacket and draped it over the bed.

"I can't believe I ran into you of all people at the dealership." Jackson said as he smiled at me.

"It's definitely a small world...I'm surprised you're even speaking to me after all the stuff that went down between us last year." I thought back to the last time I went to visit Jackson at his house and stumbled upon the fact that he was married and had a little girl. Although I found myself shocked, I couldn't be too mad at him because I was also married. It wasn't until I received that phone call from his jealous wife that completely set me off. That's why I took great joy in calling her a leaving that lovely revealing voicemail on her phone, and I thought from that point forward he would never want to speak to me again.

"Oh, you thought I was mad at you?" He asked.

"Yeah, I really did. I thought that maybe after I left that lovely little voicemail on your wife's phone that you would never want to see or speak to me again."

"No. Initially I was a little upset because I couldn't understand why you would do something like that, but the more and more I thought about it, I deserved that and probably more. I never told you I was married or had a child, and my wife was out of line for approaching you the way she did. So all is forgiven."

"I'm glad to hear that. I've wanted to reach out and apologize for that. I knew I was wrong for doing that, but I reacted out of anger. So I apologize."

"It's all good baby. I forgive you, besides we have way too much history with each other to be lying to each other in the first place."

"That's exactly how I felt."

"Ever since the last time I saw you, I've been trying to get enough nerve to contact you and make things right, but didn't think you would give me the time of day."

I laughed.

Jessica A. Robinson

"Why would you think that? You've been too good to me for me to ever do you like that."

"Well, I'm definitely glad to know this." Jackson replied and then proceeded to stare at me. I knew that stare all too well. He always looked at me like that right before we had sex. That was the infamous glare that usually started it all between us. I picked up on it immediately.

"I'm glad we got things straight so at least we're not walking around mad at each other. "I stood up from where I was sitting trying to figure out what I was going to say that would break up what I felt was getting ready to happen.

"Yeah, me too." He stood up and walked in closer to me.

"Um, I'm getting a little hungry, why don't we go and grab something to eat. *Springfield Grille* is right around the corner." I suggested as I tried to walk past him, but he ended up standing in my way so I couldn't move.

"Denise, I've missed you." He said ignoring my suggestion- all together. The way he continued to look at me caused my whole entire body to freeze up. I lost all train of thought as I began to look back at him. I could feel sweat beads beginning to form as I stood there unable to move or do anything.

"I've missed you too." I answered. I couldn't believe I had just said that!

In one instantaneous motion, Jackson began to kiss me and remove my clothing and the rest was history. I dropped my panties with the quickness and before I knew it I was completely naked and totally exhausted from our round of lovemaking.

"Mmm, Mmm, Mmm...I know I said I missed you, but I think he missed you even more." Jackson looked down at himself and then back up to me.

"Apparently, she missed you too." I smiled, but was interrupted by my cell phone ringing across the room. I jumped out of bed and scurried to answer

HOLY REVENGE

praying to God that it wasn't Randy who was calling me. I immediately picked up when I saw it was the dealership calling me instead.

"Hey, they're done with my car. I would like to take a quick shower and then we can go." I said as I pressed the end button on my phone.

"Okay, that's fine but first I was thinking we could go for round two." Jackson said as he got up from the bed and lifted me into his arms. Round two it is.

It was five in the evening when I finally made it home. I wore the biggest grin on my face. Not only had I gotten my car fixed, but I also had put an end to my circumstantial celibacy. I knew that having sex with Jackson was totally wrong, and I probably shouldn't have allowed myself to be near him, but there was another part of me that didn't feel all that guilty. I felt like if my husband hadn't cut me off completely from sex, then it wouldn't have been any room for another man to step in.

As far as I was concerned, Randy was the one that encouraged me to make a move like that. I had been trying to be the perfect wife for him and remain faithful at all cost, but I had yet to be rewarded for my efforts. I don't even really believe that he even noticed all of the hard work I had been putting into our marriage since my affair. I wouldn't even be surprised if he chose to have an affair as some sort of revenge but I know my private thoughts and reservations were absolutely ridiculous.

I knew my husband didn't have the heart to do anything like that. Before Jackson dropped me off, he stopped by the bank and withdrew money from his personal account. He blessed me with three thousand dollars. I didn't want to accept the money from him at first, but he insisted that I take it from him. I was used to more money than that, but it wasn't like I was going to turn him down.

I couldn't deny the fact that it felt good holding all that money in my hands. He kissed me and then I promised I would give him a call soon which was a complete lie, because I didn't plan on calling him at all. I know we just slept together and it may have felt like we were resuming our relationship, but that was absolutely out of the question. I made a promise to Randy that I was going to remain faithful and that's exactly what I was going to do.

As far as I was concerned, my little rendezvous with Jackson was the last time I planned on seeing him. I can't believe I was so weak and fell victim to his advances, but the more I thought about it, I always succumbed to what he wanted. Deep down inside I did feel guilty about having sex with another man, but the deed had already been done, so what was the use of crying over spilled milk?

I sat in my car parked outside in my driveway for fifteen minutes trying to wipe that stupid grin off my face so Randy wouldn't suspect anything. I couldn't help it though. My passionate tryst with Jackson had produced a giddy feeling within me and every time I thought I was cool and was about to get out the car I couldn't stop cheesing. I was smiling like I'd won the lottery. I took the money I had stuffed in my purse and put it in my glove compartment. I couldn't take the risk of Randy going in my purse and finding that wad of money sitting in there. I had finally gotten myself together enough and when I walked through the door Randy was on the floor playing with the baby.

"Hey honey. So sorry I took so long to come home, it took them a while to fix everything because they were crowded but everything is finally done now." I smiled as Randy picked up the baby and stood up to greet me with a kiss.

"It's okay babe. I understand how long those waits can be."

"Are you hungry? I'm not, but I can go and fix you something to eat." I offered.

HOLY REVENGE

"No, it's okay. Marisol ended up cooking a little something before she left and you know I have a hard time turning down her red beans and rice."

"Me either babe. I love it when she cooks. Listen, I want to apologize for how I've been acting lately. It was wrong of me to be like that toward you and I'm so sorry. I'll do whatever you want me to do in order to make this work. I scheduled my appointment with Dr. Lovett to get tested." I announced as I picked up my daughter up and gave her a big kiss. She started to giggle as I lifted her in the air and then back down in my arms.

"Thank you Denise. I'm so glad you're doing this for me. For us." He replied as he hugged me. He held me tight and wouldn't let me or the baby go. I knew my last statement was music to his ears. That is what he so desperately wanted me to do and I was tired of fighting with him. If that's what he wanted me to do then that's exactly what I was going to do. I actually couldn't wait to get to Dr. Lovett's office and get the whole ordeal over with. Then I would finally be out of the dog house with him and our life would finally be back to normal.

Chapter 12 (Denise)

"Denise I'm so glad you could make it. I really appreciate you coming." Darnell said as he opened up the door and let a huge grin appear on his face.

"I told you I would be here. I'm definitely a keeper of my word." I replied as Darnell nodded and let me and Kaylah into the house. He had called me the night before saying that he would like to meet me and possibly see the baby and I told him I would try and see what I could do. I had to end my phone conversation with him quickly while Randy was in the bathroom.

As I slept, I tried to think of a way I could meet up with him. The solution didn't come until Randy told me he was going to be a little late coming home from the church. I made up a story about going to grab a few things from the store, do a little shopping, and I was able to show up on Darnell's front door step. I was glad he lived in a secluded neighborhood and I didn't recognize anyone while I drove because Randy would kill me if he knew I was visiting Tyrone's cousin, let alone taking our daughter to see him too.

"She's absolutely beautiful." He said as he smiled at my baby and she smiled back with her friendly self.

"Thank you. I appreciate it." I replied and took a seat on his couch.

"Do you mind if I hold her?" He asked.

"No that's fine. Let me take off her jacket first." I removed her light jacket and then handed her to him.

"Wow, this is really beautiful place you have here."

"Thanks this is definitely a far cry from where I used to live and I am so glad. I lived in a complete war zone before." He shook his head from side to side and it caused me to think about the last place he resided and he wasn't lying about that one.

"It sure is. How long have you been here?" I asked.

"For about three months, you're more than welcome to take a look around if you'd like."

"Naw, maybe some other time. You said you wanted to talk to me right?" I said trying my best to stay on course for the real reason why we were there.

"Yeah, but before I talk, I want to know would you like something to drink? I have some pop and I have some wine."

"I'll take a glass of wine." I said as he handed me back my child and disappeared off into the kitchen. It had been a while since I drank anything, but I felt it was the perfect time to get a little wine up in my system. It always had a way of relaxing me and I was in need of its calming effects right about now.

As quickly as Darnell had disappeared into the kitchen, he reappeared with two wine glasses and a bottle of *Moscato* wine which was one of my wines of preference. He set the glasses down on his marble coffee table and then filled the glasses three fourths of the way.

"I have some *Moscato*, I hope that's okay."

"Yeah, it's absolutely fine." I said as he handed me the glass.

"Good, because it's all I had." He laughed.

"So, you're probably wondering why I had you come all the way over here, but I felt like some things are better said in person and there are some things we need to talk about." I took a sip from my glass and then I took a deep breath.

"If you say so." I replied. As far as I was concerned, I was perfectly fine with not discussing anything that had to do with that crazy, deranged cousin of his.

"On behalf of my cousin and my entire family, I would like to apologize for how everything went down. It was completely out of line for Tyrone to do what he did and I'm sorry that you and your family had to go through that."

"Darnell you don't have to apologize for anything. It's not like you were responsible for his behavior. That was all Tyrone's doing." I stated.

"I know I don't have to apologize, but I feel like it's the right thing to do. I mean, I loved my cousin and he was truly a brother to me, but he had some serious issues."

"So, he had mental problems?" I asked curiously. There had to be a logical explanation as to why he acted the way he did on a regular basis. I felt like at least if homeboy had some mental problems then I could justify the fact that he chose to act like a complete lunatic.

"Well, he had never been to a psychiatrist and confirmed anything, but I know he did have something. He really hadn't been right ever since his mother abandoned him and his siblings. He never truly recovered from that."

"Wow."

"I used to always tell him to go to counseling and get help so he could work through his problems, but he had told me that going to see a shrink was for crazy people and he wasn't crazy."

"So how are you handling him being gone?" I asked as I laid Kaylah down on the couch right next to me. She was fast asleep.

"I mean I'm not gonna lie. It is difficult because we were so close, but at the same time sometimes the only time some people can truly be at peace is when they're resting in peace, so I find comfort in that. He was tormented by so many things and his brothers and sisters as well."

HOLY REVENGE

"So you're trying to tell me his brothers and sisters deal with the same stuff too? Where are they?"

Hearing these things made me want to pray over my daughter right then and there. I made a mental note to anoint my daughter's head with oil as soon as we got home. I don't want none of those crazy, deranged, genes passing down to her in any way, shape, or form.

"They're scattered throughout the U.S., the only sibling that I kind of have an idea where they are is one of his baby sisters. The last I knew she was living in South Florida, but she moves so much. She's in a different state every six months and it's hard to keep up with her."

"Wow. This is a lot." I finally confessed.

"Yeah, I know this is a huge amount of information to take in but I just felt like you should know. I'm kind of glad I don't know where she is because if you thought Tyrone was crazy, then she's worse. She's a real nut case." I shook my head and then took the rest of my wine straight down in one continuous gulp. I drank it so fast that the sensation of it going down caused me to burp.

"Oops. Excuse me, I'm so sorry."

"It's okay. Would you like some more?" Darnell offered. I declined since Kaylah was with me. If I came to his house alone, I probably would've had a second and a third glass of wine.

"I'm so glad you brought the baby with you. She looks just like you." He commented and I smiled as I looked over at my little mini me.

"But the more I look at her, the more I start to see my Aunt Janice. That was Tyrone's mother."

The hell she don't, I thought as I sat there and listened to him point out certain features about my daughter that resembled certain members in their family. She doesn't look like none of them crazy people he was talking about. My daughter looked like her real family. Not none of those crazy fools.

"I'm glad you got a chance to finally see her." I simply replied. I looked down at my watch and figured it was time that we get going.

"Well, Darnell it's been real...but me and the little one must get going. I have a lot of things I have to do." I said picking my daughter up from the couch and nestled her in my arms without even waking her up.

"I'm glad you came over and we got to talk. I hope this will not be the last time."

"We'll see Darnell." I told him. I wasn't trying to make any promises. We talked for a few more minutes and then he walked me to the door. Before I walked out, I gave him a hug and told him I would call him in a few days. Darnell looked past me and had the craziest expression plastered on his face. I thought he was just trying to be silly but when I turned around I looked at what had him speechless.

My car was completely trashed! Both of the doors on my convertible were hanging wide open. I hurried over not only to find the doors open, but both of my front seats had also been ripped completely up. There was a knife stuck into my head rest and my glove compartment was open and the money Jackson had given me was all gone too. I pulled the knife out of the headrest and two things dropped onto the seat. There was a napkin from the dealership and a hotel key from the hotel I was at with Jackson! Somebody was definitely following me but who? It couldn't be Jackson because he would never do something like that to me, and my mind drew a blank when it came to thinking of anyone else.

"I can't believe this!" I said, as I looked around Darnell's neighborhood looking for a trace of anyone who was hanging around. But in fact there was no one even outside at all.

"Wow, I can't believe it either. That's crazy because I didn't hear anyone out here at all." Darnell looked around the car and then pulled out his cell phone.

HOLY REVENGE

"Who are you calling?" I asked as I saw him punching numbers into his phone.

"I'm calling the police, we have to report this."

"No! Don't call the police. I'm going to set my daughter back down on your couch real quick and make a call to someone." I replied and then went inside and called the only person I could think of calling in a situation like this and that's Terri.

When I gave Terri the address she made it there in less than ten minutes. Of course when she got to Darnell's house she was more confused than ever, but she saved all of her questions for later but that still didn't stop her from looking at me crazy.

"Terri I know you're probably thinking all kinds of crazy things right now but things are not as they seem."

"They better not be, and what is going on and why is your car a mess?" Terri asked as she took a look at my vandalized car.

"Listen, I'll explain all that to you later. but right now I just need you to take my daughter home and I'll follow you to my house."

"You mean my goddaughter is here too, where is she?" Terri asked frantically.

"Don't worry; she's on Darnell's couch asleep. I just need you to do this for me. And I'll explain everything, but when I get to the house and Randy starts drilling me with questions just let me take the lead."

I helped Terri load my daughter into her car and then I thanked Darnell for everything. As I drove to my home my mind began to run wild with all kinds of thoughts. I wondered what lie I was going to have to tell to get myself out of this one.

Chapter 13 (Randy)

"**H**ey honey, why are you coming through the front door instead of the garage door?" I asked as Denise walked in and Terri right behind her with the baby in tow. I could tell by the look on her face that something wasn't right and the fact that she didn't even say anything was starting to bother me.

"Why are you crying? You're really starting to scare me." I said as she started crying. I walked over to her and wrapped my arms around her.

"I went out to the mall to look around for a while and do some shopping for the baby and when I came back out to my car, someone had ripped up my two front seats and left the knife in my headrest and they keyed my car too. I just don't understand who would do something like this."

"What? Are you kidding me?" I asked as I could feel myself getting angry.

"No, go outside and take a look for yourself. I'm dead serious" Denise replied as I walked past them and went straight outside to see for myself. I walked around her car and opened the driver side door and looked at the seat which was completely torn into shreds. The passenger seat was also ripped up as well, and I saw the knife that they used on the floor in the front seat; and the way everything looked made me become enraged. I marched back inside the house feeling like I wanted to tear up somebody or something.

"I can't believe that someone would go to that length to vandalize a car. Did you call the police?" I asked.

"No, not yet. As soon as it happened, I called Terri because she happened to be nearby. And I figured as soon as I got home I would have you call them." Denise explained.

"Why didn't you just call me? I would've been there in five minutes flat."

"I guess I was just so scared and at the time I really couldn't think clearly. I was so scared that someone was following me that I drove away and came straight here." Denise said as she started to sob all over again.

"I'm sorry you had to go through all this honey. I just wish I was there with you when it all happened. Don't worry; we'll get everything taken care of. Terri thanks for coming to where Denise and Kaylah were. I appreciate it." I said.

"No problem Randy. Listen I'm going to take the baby upstairs and get her ready for bed." Terri said as she walked up the steps with the baby and she didn't even flinch. Denise waited until Terri took the baby upstairs before she hugged me tight.

"I'm just so glad to be home and in your arms. I was so scared baby."

"I know you were. I'm going to have one of the officers come over right now." I picked up my phone and dialed the police department and they ended up sending a cop to our front door step within twenty minutes. I didn't realize that one of the officers was one of our church members until I let them in.

"Hey Patrick, it's so good to see you. How are the wife and kids?" I asked as he reached out and hugged me and Denise.

"It's always a pleasure to see you pastor and first lady. The family is doing well. Everyone is doing great. So can you tell me what brings us out here this evening?" He asked as he pulled out his note pad. I signaled for Denise to tell the officers everything that happened. They sat and listened to her story and took notes while she talked. After giving her statement, she fixed the gentlemen a cup of coffee and they promised her that they would get to the bottom of it and catch who was responsible for messing up the car.

"Now Denise, you told me you were parked over near *Macy's* right in front of their main entrance?" Patrick asked just as he was about to walk out the door.

"Um, yeah that's where I was parked." Denise answered. She gave him a weird look and I didn't know what that was about, but maybe she was still shaken up.

"Well, I'll go down first thing in the morning and talk with the mall security staff there are several cameras throughout the parking lot and the people that messed up your car would have to be on video tape somewhere and I'll find them." Patrick replied as he gave us a hug again and then walked out of our house with his partner. I closed the door and then looked at Denise's entire countenance which appeared to be different.

"Are you okay baby?" I asked as I stared at her pale face. She looked as though she just seen a ghost.

"I'm fine Randy, I think I just need to go and lie down. It's been a long day." Denise replied as she gave me a kiss and made her way upstairs.

"Get you some rest baby. I'll be up after I let Terri out." I said as I went over to the living room and sat down on the sofa thanking God that he had kept the two most important people to me safe.

I told Denise she didn't have to worry about coming into the church to do any work for the day. Besides Tanisha was such a thorough secretary, she actually still had things pretty much taken care of for the next six months. I really missed seeing her around the church and I know once I finally caught up with my schedule that I would miss her working for me even more. I decided to log on to my computer and type a quick email to check on her.

Hey Tanisha,

HOLY REVENGE

I thought about you today as I came into the church. I hope and pray all is well at medical school. If you ever need anything please don't hesitate to call me. The church is keeping you in our prayers.
Take care and God Bless,
Pastor Randy

Just as I was getting ready to log myself out of my email I received a notification that I had a new chat message. Since I rarely get those types of messages, I decided to see who it was from:

Anonymous: Pastor please open up your eyes, your wife has been some places she has no business being. Please don't be blind to the fact that she hasn't changed. You can't teach an old dog new tricks.
I immediately typed,
Pastor Tate: Who is this?
As quickly as I typed the message was the same speed in which I received the reply.
Anonymous: Don't worry about who this is, you need to worry about what your trifling wife is doing...gotta go.

And before I could even respond the anonymous person ended our conversation just like that. This was the first time anyone had contacted me like this. *I wonder who sent me that message.* I knew someone was trying to warn me about my wife and in the past I had been blind to all the things she had been doing, but not anymore. God had allowed the dark to be exposed to the light, and ever since then my wife had been on the straight and narrow. She would have to be a fool to mess all of that up and make the same mistake twice.

However, that little anonymous message intrigued me. Even though I didn't plan on bringing it to Denise's attention, I definitely planned on keeping that piece of information in my head. I was about an hour or so into my sermon notes when my office phone rang.

"Hello, this is Pastor Tate speaking how may I help you?" I asked as I placed the phone on speaker.

"I'm so glad I caught you Pastor. It's Myra."

"Hello, how are you?"

"Oh, you know me; I'm blessed by the best so I can't complain. Listen, I was calling because I needed to talk to you about some things."

"That's fine. What seems to be on your mind?"

"Well, I been in deep prayer for quite some time just seeking God about where I needed to be and through my prayer and fasting time God has led me right back to your ministry. I feel that God is calling me to serve in your ministry."

"Are you sure about that?" I asked.

"Pastor, I've never been so sure about anything in my whole life. The way I feel now is the same way I felt when God first called me to minister eight years ago."

"So you found out about our associate minister position that we have open?"

"Yes sir. I was looking on your website and that's when I saw it, and as soon as I seen it it's like God himself spoke to me and told me to call you up. What do I have to do in order to apply?"

"Fill out the application and you can also submit your resume online as well. Once the executive board receives it, we'll have a meeting and then take a vote, and after that if you meet the qualifications then we'll fly you out and you can meet before the board. Once that happens then a final decision will be made."

"Sounds great Pastor. I'll do that today. And thanks again for this opportunity. I didn't want to hold you up on the phone so I'm gonna go but be expecting my application real soon."

"Okay, Myra, that's just fine and you have a blessed afternoon."

"I sure will. Goodbye."

HOLY REVENGE

So many people had applied and been denied for that position, it felt good to have someone who was actually qualified want to apply for the position. Yeah, we had interviewed several qualified preachers, but either they required too many things or their spirit just wasn't right. We did have a few however, who tried to get the position and hadn't even preached one sermon. It was like the more and more we advertised, the funnier the potential candidates were. So I told my executive board to pull the ad from the *Vindicator* and just post it on our website. When God wanted the position filled, He would make sure the right person saw the advertisement.

After I finished up my sermon and called a few people back to counsel with them, I packed up my briefcase and left the church. I planned to stop by my mom and dad's house and visit with them for a while but when I got over there I discovered no one was home. For a second I thought my dad was there toward the back of house in his den and maybe fell asleep, but when I walked to the back yard and looked in the window he wasn't anywhere to be found.

I should've called them before I drove all the way over here, I said to myself as I was walking back to the front of the house to my truck.

"I think your mother told me that they were going to the grocery store." Alexis said as she came out onto the porch.

"Oh, hey Alexis. I figured they must've gone somewhere. How are you?" I asked.

"I'm doing good. They just released Dad from the rehabilitation center he was in and now he's able to be with my mother at their new place."

"That's wonderful. I've been praying for him."

"Hey, if you have a few minutes can you come in for a little while. My mother gave me something to give to you." Alexis said as I walked up the walkway and into the house.

Jessica A. Robinson

"What did your mom want to give me?" I asked as Alexis went to the kitchen and came back carrying a plate.

"Guess." She smiled and then uncovered foil to reveal one of the best dishes her mother used to feed me.

"Is that your mother's chicken and dumplings?" I asked as I reached for the plate and inhaled the heavenly scent.

"Yes, it sure is. My mother was so excited that daddy was coming home today that she cooked enough food for an entire army. Once she realized she cooked too much food, she sent me with enough food to give to your family and she told me to make sure you got a plate. I was getting ready to call you and then I heard you pull up outside." Alexis explained.

"Before I forget, she also made you some chocolate chip cookies and oh, yeah, hold on one second, I almost forgot." She went over to the coffee table and picked up a stack of photo albums. She then took me by the hand and said, "Sit down."

"Are those old pictures Alexis?" I asked as I set down my plate of food. She opened the biggest album and spread it across both of our laps.

"They sure are and you're all up in here too." she laughed. We sat and began to go through all kinds of pictures from the past.

"Remember this one?" She asked as she pointed to a picture of me and her and two of our other friends that used to live on the street.

"Yeah, this is the one summer our street had the block party and we were all over Lenny's house sitting on the porch listening to tapes on his boom box."

"Yup, and look at this one." He replied.

"Isn't that from your sixteenth birthday party?" I said as Alexis nodded.

"And how can I forget this one, we took this the day..."

HOLY REVENGE

"The day I first told you I love you." I finished what she was about to say. I looked in Alexis face and she was looking back directly at me. This woman had been such a great part of my past that it was hard not to have some kind of feelings for her. Staring in her eyes reminded me so much of the past and how much I used to be in love with her, and at the same time it was a dangerous thing to be gazing into her beautiful eyes. Those same eyes got me into a lot of trouble in the past as well.

I had this incredible urge to lean in and kiss Alexis. To share the same passionate affection that we had just shared recently, but her *iPhone* rang before either of us could make a move, and I breathed a sigh of relief. It was true that when temptation was great, God would always provide a way of escape. I silently thanked Alexis's phone for being a ram in the bush because that was just what I needed to keep me out of sin. She pressed ignore on her phone, but whoever was trying to reach her called right back. She excused herself and answered the phone. Alexis went into the kitchen and began arguing with the person on the other end of the phone. I tried to listen in on what she was saying, but I couldn't really hear her. She reemerged back into the living room with tears streaming down her face.

"Alexis why are you crying?" I asked as she placed her phone down on the table and grabbed a tissue.

"I'm okay Junior, really I'm fine."

"No you're not. You're crying and I want to know what or who has made you that upset." I replied as she sat down on the couch next to me.

"Really it's no big deal. I'm okay. I just wish people would get the hint and leave me alone." She said as she closed up the photo album and replaced it on top of the stack.

"Who do you wish would leave you alone?"

"My ex-boyfriend Teddy...we've been broken up for almost four months, but he's determined to make my life a living hell. Excuse me for cussing."

"Come on Lex, this is me you're talking to. I understand you're upset."

"He calls me all day, every day, and just when I think he has finally moved on and has decided to leave me alone, he pulls a stunt like he just did."

"Well, why don't you press charges and put a restraining order out on him?" I asked.

"Easier said than done. And that's a story within itself. I just wish I never got involved with him in the first place. He's ruined my life." Alexis said as she started to cry even more and then collapsed into my arms.

"What do you mean he's ruined your life?"

"To make a long story short he's the reason why I came up here. Well, one of the reasons. I do have to help my parent's sell their house, but I had to leave Atlanta when I did because there was too much going on there."

"Like what?" I asked her sort of confused. I kind of understood what she was talking about, but on the other hand she was talking around specifics and it was hard for me to follow her completely.

"I can't really explain everything to you right now, but I promise I will tell you everything when the time is right."

I felt so bad that she had to go through such a difficult situation with someone that she couldn't get rid of and I felt even worse because there wasn't really much of anything I could do about it.

HOLY REVENGE

"**D**enise, I'm so glad you could make it into my office this afternoon. I wanted to discuss your tests results with you in person." Dr. Lovett said as she told me to have a seat.

She walked around to the other side of her desk and picked up a manila envelope that had my name labeled on it. It was something about her calling me to come into her office that didn't seem right. I had been tested for STD's in the past and I never had been asked to come into the office until today.

"So what's going on Dr. Lovett?" I asked. I just wanted her to cut to the chase and tell me the exact reason why I was there in the first place. She finally took a seat in her brown leather chair, opened the envelope, pulled out a piece of paper, and folded her hands over the document.

"Your test results came back yesterday and you are positive for Chlamydia."

"Excuse me? What did you just say?" I asked. I knew I heard what she said, but I needed her to say it one more time. She must have made a mistake.

"Your test results show that you have Chlamydia."

"That's not possible. I haven't been sleeping with anyone." I replied even though I knew that I had slept with Jackson recently. Dr. Lovett had already known so much of my business, I figured I would keep this indiscretion to myself.

"Well, even though you may not want to admit it, you can only get the disease from having unprotected sex with someone, so that's how you contracted the disease."

"So, how can it be treated?" I wanted to know what I could do to make this little problem away. If I was trying to get back into the groove with my husband, I definitely needed to eradicate this problem as quickly as possible.

"This can be treated with one shot of an antibiotic or a prescription of pills that you can take if you don't want the shot." She explained. Taking pills was out of the question because I didn't want to run the risk of Randy finding my prescription and coming to me with questions.

"I'll take the shot. Can I get it today?" I said.

"Sure. What I'll have you do is wait in the lobby for a little while, and then we'll call you to come back and I'll give you the shot, but in the meantime I want to give you some literature on practicing safe sex. Be safe out here Denise."

She handed me my results and several pamphlets on safe sex and measures to prevent sexually transmitted diseases. I honestly wanted to throw these brochures back at her, but I just took them and stuffed them inside my purse. I know I had made many mistakes in the past but she was acting like I was some dumb teenager out here sleeping with everybody. I knew what I was doing, and didn't need anyone trying to educate me on what I needed to do.

I went and sat back in the lobby where there was barely any room to begin with, but I found a seat in the corner near the window. I sat next to a young girl who looked to be no more than twenty and the minute I sat down she immediately started talking.

"Hello my name is Dionne. I'm just sitting here waiting on the doctor so I can discuss birth control options."

"Oh, that's nice." I replied. I didn't even bother telling her my name. I wasn't in the mood to make a

Jessica A. Robinson

new best friend. I was waiting on my shot so I could leave.

"Yeah, I just got the results back from my HIV test and my blood work and I'm STD free." The young woman said.

"That's great." I said as I was starting to get annoyed. I didn't know why the girl felt the need to tell me all her personal information. I wish she would just watch the television that was on or pick up a magazine and leave me alone.

"I feel it's so important to know what your status is concerning STD's because there's so many people walking around who have something and don't even know it or they won't get checked."

"You're right about that." I answered and then I picked up the *Essence* magazine that was lying on the coffee table. I hoped she would get the hint that I really didn't care to hold a conversation with her and just be quiet. God must've heard my thoughts because the nurse called her name just as she was about to say something else to me. I silently thanked God that she was leaving, and I also thanked God that she left behind her paper that stated she was completely free and clear of any disease. I planned on using that to my advantage.

When I pulled into the parking lot of the church, I was on a mission. I planned on going straight into my office and recreating the document that I had taken from the doctor's office. I was glad to see there weren't too many cars in the parking lot, that way there would be less people for me to have to stop and talk to. I was in such a rush that when I walked in the building I walked past Kenny's desk without even saying hello. I didn't even know he was there.

"Oh, so you're gonna walk past me and not say anything?" Kenny said, as he got up from where he was sitting and followed me the entire way to my office.

"Kenny, I have a lot of things on my mind. I didn't mean to do that. I'm sorry." I said quickly hoping that answer would be sufficient enough and wouldn't warrant an entire conversation.

"What's on your mind? I can tell you what's on my mind. I'm thinking about all the freaky things I could do to you if you would only let me." He answered.

Kenny never ceased to amaze me. He always had something obnoxiously inappropriate to say to me at any given moment. It's like this man had absolutely no shame.

"I can't believe you insist on talking to me like that when you know my husband is here and probably can hear you." I smiled. When I mentioned my husband, he always had this uncomfortable look on his face. It made me snicker a little.

"Why you always have to bring him up? I'm not worried about your beloved husband, besides he's in his office with his door closed and he said he didn't want to be disturbed. He was on the phone with somebody." Kenny explained.

"I bring him up because he's the reason why you have job now, and I know the church pays you good, so you better be careful and not bite the hand that feeds you. You might end up injured and broke." I said as I dropped my purse onto my desk and then turned on my computer.

"Oh, is that supposed to scare me? I'm the best security guard this church has ever seen and I'm not going anywhere. I wish you would just be honest with yourself and being in denial."

"Denial about what?"

"Denial about what you need."

"You're so funny. If you're so smart and you think you know what I need then what is it?"

"I know what you've been missing and I'd rather show you rather than tell you." Kenny said as he moved in closer to me and brushed up against me from behind. The man just wouldn't give up. Not only did he rub up against me, but he pressed his body into mine until there was no space between us and let me get a quick feel of what he was talking about. I started to pray a quick prayer because at that moment, him letting me feel what he was working with was surely evil, and was about to lead me straight into temptation. I needed Jesus to intervene that very second because confident sexy men were my weakness, and right then Kenny fit the bill. I stepped away from him and moved around to the other side of my desk. I tried my best to act like what he did didn't affect me, but that was far from the actual truth. Kenny was about to have me sweating before too long.

"You know I'm what you need. You can only fight for so long, might as well do what feels good to you." Kenny attempted to kiss me when I quickly moved and caused him to fall on my desk. He started to laugh.

"You're quick there I see." He said as he stood up, and I laughed at him because he looked absolutely ridiculous.

"I'm too quick." I smiled.

"It's okay. You may have won this time around but it's only a matter of time until I'll have you screaming my name."

"Don't count on it. Goodbye Kenny." I said as I pointed to the door and didn't say anything else until he left my office. I got myself situated and then I proceeded to recreate a document that looked just like the one I borrowed from my doctor's office. Once I was convinced that it was a perfect duplicate, I printed out a copy and tore the old one up. I placed the new piece of paper in my purse and then I left my office to go and see my honey. I know Kenny said that Randy didn't want to be disturbed, but that rule definitely didn't apply to me. I knocked lightly on his door until I heard him say, "Come in."

"Hey baby, are you busy? I just wanted you to know that I just came back from the doctor's office and..." Before I could finish what I was about to say Randy cut me off.

HOLY REVENGE

"I was busy, but I'm not anymore. You're actually just the person I wanted to see. Close the door." He replied as I closed the door and sat across from him.

"What's up baby?" I asked as I looked at his facial expression which had me sort of confused. He appeared as though he was angry about something.

"So Patrick called me today and we had a little talk about the security footage from the mall. He informed me that there wasn't any footage of you at the mall on the day your car was vandalized, nor was there any footage of your Mercedes anywhere in the parking lot. So you tell me what's going on because something doesn't seem right to me."

"What do you mean? I was at the mall when I said I was. I don't care if Patrick is saying I was on camera or not. I was there and my car was vandalized in that parking lot. Why do you think I'm lying?" I asked him as I crossed my arms.

"Denise come on...he said he reviewed every camera at every angle he could inside the mall and out in the parking lot and you or your red car never made an appearance. So you tell me who's lying?"

"I can't believe that you would think I'm lying. For all you know I could've been attacked by some crazed madman and your daughter was in danger and all you could think about is the fact that I'm not on some camera."

"I don't mean to sound like I'm heartless and I don't care, but I just feel in my spirit that you are not being honest with me and I want to know where you were for real."

I was getting ready to say something when he added, "And before you open up your mouth to lie to me again, please remember you're in the house of the Lord and it would behoove you to tell the truth."

"Randy, I was at the mall. I don't have to lie to you. I have no reason to. Now, if you choose to believe me that's your choice, but I'm not going to sit here and have you treat me like I'm some guilty child when I know I'm innocent." I replied.

"Denise I pray that you are telling me the truth, because if you're not...then the truth will come out sooner or later. If you'll excuse me, I have to finish up the last minute travel plans so Myra can come and be interviewed by the executive board in two days."

Randy turned toward his computer and acted as though I wasn't even there. Here I was trying to come and tell Randy that we had the green light to resume our sex life, and he wanted to destroy my celebratory mood because he thinks I'm lying. It didn't matter about all the hard work I had just put in so that me and Randy could get back to the way we used to be, this new revelation took us back to square one...again!

HOLY REVENGE

Chapter 15 (Terri)

I must've called Carlos twenty times in the past two days and he has yet to return my phone calls. I know he was a busy man and had a lot going on, but he usually took the time to call me and at least let me know what was going on. I hadn't even gotten a text message in two days. I was beginning to get worried. I usually wasn't bothered when I didn't hear from him, but having absolutely no communication with him even for that short amount of time made me somewhat nervous and concerned.

I found myself being unable to concentrate all morning while I was at work. Thank God I didn't have to see any clients and I didn't have any court dates because by noon, I had packed up my *Gucci* briefcase and told my colleagues that I would be working the rest of the day from home. I was starting not to feel good even though I knew I wasn't coming down with anything. I think it was more of my nerves than anything else. I stopped by Carlos' house on my way home to my condo and I knocked on his door. Maybe he had stopped home for something on his lunch break and I could catch him there. When I pulled up to his house, he wasn't home. I could tell he wasn't there because the garage was down and all the lights were off in his house. I looked in his mailbox and there was a huge stack of mail piled up and that was unlike him because he usually always picked up his mail as soon as he came home from work.

I pulled out my cell phone and dialed his number. I ended up getting sent straight to voicemail so I left him a message:

> *Hey baby, it's me. I've been trying*
> *to reach you for the past two days*
> *and you haven't called me back.*
> *When you get this message, please*
> *give me a call. I love you.*

I ended my call and then got back in my car and drove home where I changed into a black *Bebe* sweat suit. I lounged around the whole day and finished preparing a few documents for two upcoming cases I had and then I decided to watch a few movies.

After I watched *Love and Basketball* and *Brown Sugar,* I realized that Carlos still hadn't returned any of my messages. I picked up my phone to dial him again when I accidentally dialed Denise's cell phone number.

"Hey, Terri what's up?" Denise said.

"Hey, I was trying to call Carlos but I dialed you instead. What are you up to today?" I asked as I picked up the remote and turned off the television.

"Absolutely nothing. My mom and stepdad came and got Kaylah and took her back to Columbus for two weeks so I got all the free time in the world. And Randy and I aren't getting along at the moment so I really have time to myself."

"Oh, Lord, what's going on now?" I asked.

"Are you busy; because it's a long story?"

"No, I'm actually at home doing nothing so you can stop by if you want." I replied.

"I'll be over in the next five minutes; I'm not too far from your house." Denise said as we hung up with each other. I went downstairs and logged back into my computer that was in my office and checked my emails. Carlos hadn't even sent me an email. I was really starting to get worried so I sent him a simple email that said:

> *Hey Baby, I haven't heard from you*
> *in a few days. I'm starting to get worried*
> *because you haven't returned any of my*
> *phone calls or text messages. When you*
> *get this email and I know you'll get it*

soon because it comes straight to your phone, please send me something to let me know that you're okay. I love you Carlos.

"What are you doing sending love notes to your man?" Denise asked as she came into my office and scared the living daylights out of me. I'd forgotten I gave her a key when I first purchased my home in case she needed to come here for anything.

I jumped. "You scared me half to death." I said as I took a deep breath and got off the internet.

"I can't understand for the life of me why you gave me a key if you never expect me to use it."

"It's not like I don't expect you to use it, but I guess you just caught me off guard. I was sending Carlos an email. I haven't heard or seen him in two days."

"And that's odd coming from him?"

"Yeah because we talk and see each other every day. I've called him like thirty times, stopped by his house, and I just emailed him and I haven't heard anything."

"Have ya'll had an argument or been fighting about anything?"

"Not at all. We've pretty much been the same. And the last night we saw each other we went out to dinner and although he was acting a little different, we still had a good time."

"What you mean he was acting different?"

"I don't know. He was acting like he was down about something. He was quieter than he usually is. And when I asked him what was wrong, he said he really didn't want to talk about it."

"Maybe he's just going through something and needs a little space."

"That may be true, but he's never gone this long without at least letting me know he's okay. I'm worried Denise. Hopefully he'll get all my messages tonight and I'll hear from him soon." Denise followed me to my mini bar and I fixed us both a glass of wine. This was

HOLY REVENGE

definitely a moment that we needed a little something to help us ease up a bit.

"Yeah, you'll hear from him before you know it."

"So what's going on between you and Randy now?"

"Girl, what isn't going on between us? Well, I went to be tested and like I figured, I didn't have anything. I went to take the good news to my husband so I can finally get out of the dog house with him, and he hits me with the news that Patrick, the cop, looked at all the surveillance footage from the mall and I'm not anywhere to be found in any of the footage."

"Well, you weren't at the mall to begin with so he would be correct in bringing that information to you. Why won't you just tell him you were over Darnell's house so he can know the truth?"

"Why? So I can be killed? Randy has forbidden me to keep in touch with any of Tyrone's family members and Darnell is Tyrone's cousin."

"Oh...so what did else did he say?"

"He told me he could feel I was lying and he wanted me to stop because he wanted to know the real truth but I stood my ground. I told him I don't care if Patrick didn't see me anywhere on camera, I was still at the mall and that was it. He hasn't spoken to me since and you know what? Right now, I don't even care. I'm tired of trying to be this perfect person and he doesn't even notice. I'm back to doing me all the way."

"Oh, wow. So you think that is the solution to all of your problems you're having? Just go back to doing you huh? You don't think you and Randy need to go to marital counseling?"

"That's the only thing I can think of right now. I used to have so much fun when the only person I was thinking about was me and right now that's what I plan to do. Besides we're not going to some overpriced counselor that's only going to create more problems for us"

"Suit yourself Denise, but I don't think that's going to solve anything. It will only make things worse. I'm just worried that this time something might happen that you won't be able to bounce back from."

"Don't worry about me at all. Randy will come to his senses sooner or later, and I hope it's sooner because there's no telling what I will do given the opportunity and chance."

"Oh my God…I know what you're getting at and I'll be praying for you, because that could only mean one thing." I replied as Denise guzzled her last sip of wine and then pushed her glass back to me.

"Yeah, give me another glass of your finest." Denise said as I shook my head and granted her request.

HOLY REVENGE

Chapter 16 (Randy)

I couldn't understand for the life of me why Denise felt the need to lie to me after all this time. When she had initially came home and claimed her car was vandalized at the mall I believed her until I thought about her entire story and saw how things really didn't add up. Regardless of how I felt about her story, I still decided to believe her and stand by her through the whole situation; but when Patrick called to tell me that she wasn't on any of the camera footage I was furious!

Not only did she lie and try to play me, but she still insisted on lying even though I knew she wasn't telling the truth. That's what made me upset. And then my mind got to thinking, if she lied about that situation what else was she lying about?

That was a hard place to be in not being able to trust my very own wife, but I'm just trying to keep it real. I was really trying to move from the whole infidelity thing but it seemed like I was still in the same place. I haven't even spoken to her since the day she lied to me at the church. I don't even know what to say. I opened my Bible and began to study about renewing my mind with the Word of God and that's exactly what I needed to do. I got on my knees in my home office and began to pray to the Lord.

Lord, I come to you the best way I know how and I'm asking that you help me get through this situation with Denise. I don't trust anything she says or does and I really don't wanna be like that so please help me to have a forgiving heart and to love her with the love of Christ. In Jesus name, amen.

When I got up from saying my prayer, I received a call from Denise saying that she wasn't going to be home any time soon which didn't bother me because I wasn't really in the mood to see her anyway. I told her that was fine and we hung up. I didn't even bother to ask her where she was going or what she was doing. At this point, I wasn't even really concerned because if she couldn't tell me the truth, I would rather her not say anything at all.

Marisol had ended up cooking me a little something before she went home, and I was glad that I didn't have to heat up a microwave dinner or go and grab any fast food because I wasn't in the mood for that either. I heated up a plate of baked chicken, macaroni and cheese, and sat at the dining room table by myself and enjoyed my dinner in silence. It felt good to just be alone and not have to ignore someone on purpose.

After I was done, I decided to call my mother and check up on her.

"Hey son, what's going on?" My mother said all joyous on the other end of the phone. She always had a happy disposition that made me smile even on my worst day.

"Nothing much mom. I was just calling to see what you and dad were up to."

"Same old stuff, different day son. You know how it is." She replied and then let out a chuckle. She was probably referring to the fact that she was catching up on her soaps and my dad was in his eternal chill spot—his den.

"Yeah, I know exactly what you mean." I answered.

"What's wrong Randy?" My mother asked me.

"Nothing is wrong. Why?" I forgot my mother was an expert at interpreting my voices and knew when something was wrong with me.

"Come on son. Now you know, I know you better than you know yourself, and I can tell when something is going on so what's up?" She asked.

"Denise and I aren't really seeing eye to eye on some things that's all. I've been praying about it though."

"And that's the best thing you can do son. I'm not trying to be all up in your business and I don't even want to know but you're doing the right thing. Prayer changes things, and you have to just ask God to bring a resolution to the issues ya'll are having. You pray, and I guarantee that God will show you how to handle the situation and it will all work out."

"Thanks mom. I really appreciate it but I just don't know what's going to happen between us. I've been praying not only for things to be resolved, but if there's anything that I need to find out, that God will reveal it to me."

"God will do that too, so be ready for whatever it is. Good or bad." My mother replied.

"You're right about that one. Well, I didn't want to hold you but I just wanted to call and see how you were doing. I'll catch up with you soon."

"Okay baby, talk to you later bye." My mother said and I hung up the phone. You can definitely tell my mother has grown because in the past she would've probably told me to divorce that hussy and don't think twice, but here she was encouraging me to pray and wait for God to change things.

I spent the rest of my evening watching *ESPN* and catching up on all the games I missed during the week. I was getting ready to go to bed when Alexis sent me a text message.

> *Alexis: Hey Junior what's up?*
> *Me: Nothing much, about to get ready for bed. U?*
> *Alexis: You were on my mind and thought I would check in and see how you were doing.*

HOLY REVENGE

Me: That was sweet of you. I'm good. Can't complain at all.
Alexis: Listen, I didn't mean to bother you, but I would like to thank you for being there the other day when I got that phone call. I appreciate it more than you ever know.
Me: Aww, don't mention it. I was glad I was able to be there. You don't have to thank me. That's what friends are for.
Alexis: Well, thanks for being an awesome friend. Your wife is such a lucky woman to have a man like you. Have a good night.
Me: Goodnight Alexis.

I'm not even going to lie. Alexis always knew how to make me smile; the fact that we were now grown adults didn't change that fact. I put my phone on silent, plugged it into its charger and went to bed with a huge grin on my face.

When I woke up the next morning, I noticed Denise had come in and was still sleep next to me. I didn't know what time she came home, because by the time I went to sleep at one in the morning, she still hadn't made it home. I let the alarm sound a few extra minutes while I picked out what I was going to wear. Denise finally rolled over to my side of the bed and pounded her fist on the off button.

"You didn't hear the alarm going off for that long?" She asked me, obviously annoyed that I just let it keep sounding without turning it off.

"I heard it Denise, I just didn't have a chance to shut it off that's all. But thank you though." I replied.

"I was trying to sleep until that thing woke me up out of my sleep. I don't even know if I'll be able to go back at all."

"Well, if you knew how to come in this house at a decent hour, then you wouldn't be so tired now would you?" I stated as I stared directly in her face.

"Excuse me? Since when did you become my daddy? If I want to come in the house late, then that should be my business, not yours, besides I didn't even come in late if that's what you're referring to. I was just at Terri's house if you must know. Daddy...what are you gonna ground me? Did I break the rules again?" Denise said as she began to laugh. I didn't see anything funny.

"What are you talking about? I'm not trying to control when you come and go, but I just don't understand how you feel like you can do whatever you want, like you're single, coming in this house all late and not telling me where you're going, and I'm supposed to be fine with that? I don't think so. I don't know what has gotten into you, but we really need to sit down and talk about everything and real soon."

"Well, why don't we talk now since you're stupid alarm clock woke me up. I have all the time in the world now. I think right now would be the perfect time." Denise sat up in bed and crossed her arms.

"We will have to talk later. Today is the day Myra has her interview with the executive board. I have to hurry up before I'm the one that's late, but we will talk. Believe that." I said as I gathered my things and went into the bathroom to get ready for the day.

"Oh, yeah, I forgot about that. Well, I'll be going shopping, so I guess we can talk tonight when I get back home."

Instead of asking her why she felt the need to go shopping I just answered, "That'll be fine."

I couldn't understand why she wanted to go shopping when practically her entire closet was full of brand new designer clothes with the price tags still on them, but that was what she always did.

"Pastor Randy, I'm so nervous about this interview today. My mind has been racing all morning." Myra said as she sat across from me in my office. We were waiting for the executive board to assemble so we could start the formal interview. She came into my office and paced back and forth a few times before I

HOLY REVENGE

finally suggested that she have a seat and relax a little. I knew the interview process could be quite nerve wracking, but I knew she would do well.

"Myra just take some deep breaths and just relax. Everything will be okay. I promise you."

"I know, I know. But what if I clam up and can't respond properly to what is asked of me?"

"I honestly don't think that is gonna happen. You're more qualified for this position than anybody who has applied. And remember, God has not given you the spirit of fear, so go into this interview with boldness and claim it like you already have it." I smiled at her and she smiled back at me.

"Thank you so much. I really appreciate that. I'm ready now." Myra stood up and one of the board members opened the door to my office and said, "We're ready for you. You can come now."

"I guess I spoke that into existence!" She laughed.

"How do I look?" She asked before she walked out. I was tempted to say she looked like she fell off one of the pages of my favorite magazines, but I felt that might go too far so I just simply answered. "You look just fine."

"Thank you." She replied. Myra was dressed to kill in a black church suit that had to be tailor made because it fit every nook and cranny of her body just perfect. When she had first walked into my office I did a double take and had to remember to get my eyes together and back focused before she figured that I was staring at her. But she looked phenomenal to say the least.

Once we arrived in the conference room they asked Myra to sit in a chair they provided for her and the executive board and I sat in a panel style in the front of the room. The board wasted no time in asking her questions and one after one she answered them like a true professional. I was so impressed in how she handled herself. She didn't even break into a sweat or

Jessica A. Robinson

appear nervous at all. She was able to answer everything that they asked and by the end of interview even the couple skeptical board members we had were in complete awe of Myra.

"Pastor, do you have any questions for Minister Myra before we close this interview?" Deacon Russell said as the entire room focused their attention on me.

"You know what? I think everyone has pretty much asked what I wanted to ask, so I believe we're done here." I stated.

"Myra do you have anything else to say before we conclude this interview?" I turned to Myra and asked her.

"Yes, I do. I would like to thank the entire executive board and you Pastor Randy for giving me the opportunity to even have the interview and even if I don't get the position as the new associate minister, I have still been blessed by this ministry. Thank you."

"You're welcome Myra. We appreciate you for flying in from Atlanta to come here for this interview. The board will have a quick meeting and we will inform you of our decision tomorrow. We have one of the drivers waiting to take you back to your hotel, so please enjoy the rest of your day and we will speak with you in the morning."

The board came back into my office and discussed the entire interview over and while most were on board to hire Myra for the position there were a few of our "old school" members who felt like a woman had no business being in the pulpit. After a few minutes of back and forth debating, all of the other members, including myself, were able to convince the two who were opposed to hiring her, to see it from our point of view. Since they prided themselves in our ministry being on the cutting edge and always staying a step ahead of the rest, they saw the benefits of adding a female to our all male ministerial staff.

"So our meeting is adjourned. It looks like we have just found ourselves our newest associate

HOLY REVENGE

minister. I can't wait to announce this news to the entire congregation tomorrow during Sunday morning service."

Jessica A. Robinson

Chapter 17 (Denise)

"To what do I owe this honor?" Kenny asked as he opened up the door to his loft apartment on the west side.

"Please don't act surprised to see me. You just sent me a text message after church that had your address and invitation inside." I said as I walked past him and into his place. Kenny smiled and then laughed and then proceeded to shut the door behind me.

Normally, I wouldn't have paid any attention to what he was saying, but after the service we had today I was beyond pissed. His text message came at a time when I just needed to get out of the house, so when he sent it to me I just got into my car and drove to his place without a second thought. Church service was going on as it always does and Randy came up in the pulpit like he was about to preach but instead he decided to make an announcement:

> Well, after long deliberation and search for an associate minister to join our staff and church family, I'm pleased to announce that the search is over and I would like for Oakdale to welcome Myra Washington as the new addition to our ministry.

My mouth dropped open as Myra stepped out onto the platform and stood next to my husband in the pulpit. I knew she had flown in town to have her interview before the executive board, but I wasn't aware that they had already made their final decision. I looked up at my husband, who looked back at me and smiled, but in turn I rolled my eyes and turned my head in the opposite direction. I couldn't believe he hired that heifer without even telling me. From that moment on I didn't even want to be in the service at all. I would've rather be at home than in church.

After church was dismissed, I gathered my things and went into Randy's office and waited for him. I know that I was supposed to stand in the sanctuary and greet everybody, but today I found myself just not being in the mood at all. My attitude was at an all-time high and if someone came to me and said the wrong thing, I might be liable to go off on somebody. I knew it wouldn't be long before Randy came into his office trying to figure out what was going on with me.

Like clockwork Randy stormed into his office and locked his door. I looked at him and could tell he was mad but at that moment I honestly didn't care.

"What's wrong with you Denise? I saw how you were looking at me at the end of service and please don't sit here and play like you are fine because I know you're not."

"I was looking at you because I don't understand how you make decisions like you do and don't even bother to tell me." I said as I rolled my eyes and crossed my arms.

"So this is about Myra coming on as associate minister isn't it?" Randy asked.

"I just don't understand how she just came in town yesterday and she already has the job. How did you pull that off? I know there were a few members who were against it."

"The entire board was in agreement that Myra is the perfect person for the job and she will be a great addition to our staff to kind of mix things up a little."

"I bet..." I laughed.

"What's that supposed to mean?"

"Absolutely nothing Randy. Are you ready to go? I'm tired and I just want to get home." I glanced down at my watch. I was done with Randy and this stupid conversation we were having.

Jessica A. Robinson

"Well, the ministers and I were talking while we were in the sanctuary, and we all decided to take Myra out to dinner with our families."

"You've got to be kidding right?" I asked.

"No, that's what we all just decided. We're going to all meet out at *Olive Garden.*"

"Well, I don't wanna go and I'm not hungry at all. Just take me home." I replied.

"But Denise, everyone is going all the ministers and their wives."

"I don't care. Tell them I don't feel well. I don't wanna go and I would appreciate if you would take me home. Thank you."

Finally Randy threw up his hands.

"Whatever Denise. If home is where you want to go I'll take you. Let's go." Randy said as he grabbed his keys and I followed right behind him out of the church.

"I can't believe you're here at my place. Denise Tate in the flesh, I'm definitely a lucky man right now." Kenny smiled from ear to ear.

"I can't believe I'm here either, but I guess life is full of surprises." I said as he motioned for me to sit on his black leather couch. He sat on one end and I sat on the other. My eyes scanned around his place and I was impressed with how he had everything set up. With him having such a beat up car I figured his place wasn't up to par, but I was pleasantly surprised.

"Why are you sitting all the way over there? I won't bite you. Unless you ask me to." He winked as he scooted in a little closer to me. He picked up a remote and pressed play on his *iPod* and some Jill Scott started playing softly in the background.

"What you know about Jill Scott?" I asked as I placed my purse down on his coffee table.

"A lot. She's one of my favorite neo-soul artists." He answered.

"Me too."

HOLY REVENGE

"So what made you invite me over today?" I was curious to see what made him reach out to me today out of all days.

"I saw how upset you were after church and I thought today might be a good day to reach out and try to get you to come over. Why did you accept? You've been turning all my offers down since the first time I met you." He laughed.

"Well, today was just one of them days where I needed a break. A change of scenery so to speak, so you reached out at the right time."

"What has you so upset Denise? You too sexy to be that stressed and upset." He smiled and then cracked open a bottle of *Mimosa* and poured me a glass.

"Thank you. I absolutely love *Mimosa*. I haven't had some in so long; I almost forgot how it tasted." I said as I took a long sip of the mixture and closed my eyes as I savored its unique taste.

"I usually don't drink it that much, but I thought you might like it that's why I stopped and purchased a bottle earlier."

"Good choice...good choice." I smiled.

"So you never answered my question either. What has you so upset? You can tell me." He replied.

"I rather not get into all of that, but I am upset though and I just need a break for real." Even though I was willing to admit that I was upset, I wasn't willing to disclose the real reason why I was mad. And I definitely wasn't trying to spill the beans about Randy and I having problems even though he probably suspected that.

"Well, please let today be a time of rest and relaxation. Here I'll pour you some more." He said as filled my glass back up so that it was full. I sipped on my lovely drink as Kenny switched back and forth between songs on his playlist. I smiled as he settled on a Anthony Hamilton song.

"Your playlist sounds a lot like mine." I commented.

"What? You mean your playlist isn't boggled down with all the gospel greats and negro spirituals and hymns?" He laughed.

"Of course not. I have a few gospel albums, but I mostly have R&B on my *iPod*. I know I'm the first lady, but I still enjoy my music."

"And that is why I like you, because you're down to earth. You don't try to put on a front for nobody. You're just you and that's why I'm attracted to you." Kenny said as he put down his glass and moved directly next to me on the couch. I could smell his *Polo* cologne as he got close to me.

"You are so beautiful; you know that? I know you have a hard time taking me seriously because I'm always flirting with you at the church. But you are really a beautiful woman."

"Thank you Kenny."

"And although you don't really want to tell me why you're so upset; it's okay. I just know that if I was blessed enough to have a woman like you, that you would always have a smile on your face."

"Whatever...you're just saying that." I said and then Kenny gently turned my face toward him.

"No, I mean that. If you were mine I would treat you like the queen that you are. Randy doesn't know what he has." Kenny replied.

Well, I definitely agreed with Kenny's last statement. Randy didn't know what he had because if he did, then I wouldn't have to jump through hoops just to please him. I felt like every day I was on trial and had all this work to do just to try and get his attention, but I was tired of Randy and all his demands. It was time to start playing by my own rules.

Kenny leaned in and brought his lips to mine and we shared the most passionate kiss. It was so intense that it brought chills up and down my spine. It didn't take long before he led me to his bedroom and

HOLY REVENGE

showed me just exactly what he'd wanted to do to me for such a long time. He practically was able to run circles around any other man that I had been with. I was barely able to catch my breath.

"I know I may sound greedy right now, but that was so good I'm ready for the second round." Kenny said as he kissed the top of my right shoulder and then positioned himself right next to me.

"Good isn't even the word to describe what just went down. I honestly don't think there's a word in the dictionary to articulate that." I replied as I smiled from ear to ear. To say that Kenny was good at what he does, would be a complete understatement. He was great at pleasuring a woman and I would have to say sex was among his best qualities. Even though I was in a present state of euphoria, I still felt guilty though. I didn't expect to actually have sex with Kenny. I wasn't trying to give in, but he made it so hard for me not to that I really didn't have a fighting chance.

"Even though you tried to play hard to get, I knew you wanted me just as much as I wanted you."

"Oh, is that right?" I asked as I laughed.

"Yeah, I can see straight through your little tough act, and it's all good." Kenny said.

"Whatever. You think you know me so well, but you don't know anything at all."

"So answer me this. When will I get another chance to hook up with you again?" Kenny asked. Although I wanted to say tomorrow and the next day, I knew that was unrealistic and besides, I wasn't trying to start anything with him anyway. God had already delivered me from one crazy psycho and I wasn't taking any applications for a new one.

"I honestly don't know Kenny. I think it would be best if we played everything by ear." I answered. I knew that wasn't what he wanted to hear, but I was trying to be as honest as I could.

"I'm perfectly fine with that. I agree that's what's best too." Kenny replied, as I smiled and then climbed on top of him. I was going to give him exactly what he asked for before I decided to go home. He wanted round two and that's exactly what he was going to get.

HOLY REVENGE

Chapter 18 (Randy)

"Thanks for meeting me Junior. I really appreciate it." Alexis said as she sat across from me at *Rachel's Restaurant.*

"Of course. I wasn't doing anything and I was getting hungry, so you called at the perfect time." I was at the church staring at my sermon notes when she called and invited me to lunch. She provided me with the perfect excuse to leave the church early and forget about where in the world my wife was.

"Is your wife okay with you meeting me out for lunch? I don't want to cause any problems."

"Oh, don't worry she's fine with everything." I reassured her. Besides me being out to lunch with Alexis wouldn't create any more problems than we already had. We still hadn't talked about anything and lately it seemed like my wife was acting like she was single. Coming and going as she pleased, not answering her phone, and still lying about where she had been. I had been trying my best to be patient with her and remain calm, but my patience was definitely wearing thin.

"Are you okay? You seem like you're stressed about something." Alexis said as she took a sip of her water.

"I'm okay. Denise and I are going through a little something, but I know we'll get through it." I answered.

"I've never been married, but I do know that it's a lot of work. Your wife seems like she's a nice woman. As long as you two meet in the middle and compromise some things, everything will work out." Alexis said as the waitress brought out her Caesar salad and my cup of lobster bisque soup.

"Thanks Alexis. Well, enough about me, what's going on with you?" I asked.

"Well, that's why I wanted to meet you out for lunch. I wanted to tell you in the person that I have to go back to Atlanta. I have so many things that I have to do and get straight that I'm leaving tomorrow morning."

"What's up? Did you already sell your parent's house?" I asked.

"No. Not yet, but I have to go and tie up some loose ends with my ex. Teddy is trying to sabotage my name and my business. I met him almost two years ago and we began dating shortly after we met. After about six months he started talking about getting married and we were moving toward spending our lives together. At the time, I was just getting my dental office off the ground and he was very supportive. Trying to do whatever he could to help me.

He gave me a large amount of money to put into my business from his restaurant that he owned, and everything was fine until one day the police came to my business looking for him. Long story short, he's in trouble with the feds and he's trying to take me down with him, but I had no idea he was selling drugs. When he went in to court and they questioned him about who was working for him, he let my name escape from his lips and that's where my trouble all started." Alexis explained and started crying.

I pulled my handkerchief from my suit and handed it to her so she could wipe her eyes. I never knew she was going through such a difficult situation. I felt so bad that she even had to go through something like that.

"So, what's happening with the courts and what is the judge saying?"

"Well, they shut my practice down until further notice and they're investigating me. I was doing so good for myself down in Atlanta until all of this happened. I just feel like my life is so messed up. I feel all alone." Alexis said.

"You're not alone Lex. You have so many people who are in your corner including me. If you need a good lawyer, my wife's best friend is the best attorney in this city and she should be able to point you in the right direction. I'll give you her number before we leave."

"Thank you so much. I really appreciate that. It's like you always have all the answers."

"While I don't claim to have all the answers, I know a man who does. I would like to pray with you." I grabbed a hold of both of her hands and prayed for her right in the middle of the restaurant. I didn't care who was watching me.

"Thanks for praying Randy. I know everything will be alright."

"You're welcome. And although you're leaving, if you ever need me don't hesitate to call. I'm here for you." I gave Alexis a hug before we both left and went our separate ways. So much for my few moments of peace and tranquility.

When I came home from my lunch with Alexis, Denise was sitting in the living room waiting on me like I had been out all night, but it was only three in the afternoon.

"So, where were you? I came down to the church because I wanted to bring you some lunch and you weren't anywhere to be found, and Kenny had no idea where you went."

"I left early because I had to be somewhere. And why are you questioning me? You seem to never have an answer when I ask you where you've been." I replied, as I sat down my briefcase and loosened my tie. Her eyes focused in on my handkerchief that was sticking out of my pocket further than usual.

HOLY REVENGE

"Is that lipstick on your hanky?" Denise asked as she got up from where she was sitting and pulled it completely out of my pocket.

"Yes, that's lipstick." I answered. There was no way I could deny the bright pink lipstick that Alexis had worn at the restaurant earlier.

"So, you go missing in action and then you come home with lipstick on your hanky? Who's lipstick is this Randy?"

"Why does that matter Denise?"

"Because I want to know. Who does this lipstick stain belong to?"

I took a deep breath and braced myself before I answered, "Alexis."

Just hearing her name sent my wife to another level of anger.

"What the hell are you and Alexis hanging out for?"

"Why are you jumping to conclusions Denise? Alexis and I aren't hanging out, I went to lunch with her today because she's leaving to go home tomorrow, but you're so worried about what I'm out there doing that you wouldn't understand that. But let's talk about what you're out there doing since you want to act like you haven't done anything at all."

"There's nothing for me to talk about. I'm just tired of you always hanging what I've done over my head like I'm some bad person. I know I'm not perfect, and I know I've made mistakes, but I'm trying to do better and turn over a new leaf, but it seems like you don't see that or even care." Denise said as she started to cry. I didn't care how mad I was at her at that point; I hated to see her cry and I realized that our fighting and arguing back and forth wasn't solving anything.

"Look Denise, I didn't know you felt that way. I have been taking notice that you've been trying, but marriage is hard work and in order for it to work, we both must agree to meet in the middle and work on things together. In order to get back to a good place, we have to stop fighting and make up. And I know just what we need to do in order to start." I said as I wiped the tears from her face. I took her by the hand and then she asked, "Where are we going?"

"We're going upstairs to our bedroom." I winked, and then I carried her up the steps. It was time for us to stop fighting once and for all.

HOLY REVENGE

Chapter 19 (Terri)

It had been two weeks since I had seen or heard from Carlos and I was beyond worried. I didn't know what to think. Maybe he had gotten hurt and nobody knew to contact me. Maybe there was a death in the family and he had to fly home and be with his family. Maybe he was a certified criminal and was locked away in a federal prison. Whatever it was, I was still in the dark and didn't have a clue as to what happened to him. Instead of calling him a million times a day like I was tempted to, I only called twice a day. I figured if he hadn't answered my first phone call there was no way he was going to answer my one hundredth phone call.

For the first week after he disappeared, I was unable to really function. I couldn't eat, I couldn't sleep, and work was the furthest thing from my mind. I missed so many days in one week that my colleagues thought I had lost a loved one, but in my heart I felt like I really had lost someone dear to me. It felt as though someone I loved dearly had died because I still hadn't heard from Carlos.

My mind raced day and night trying to come up with a story of what could have happened to him, but the more I thought about him, the more frustrated I became. Why couldn't he just call me back? Why couldn't he just email me and let me know that he was alright. That's all I wanted. He didn't have to give me some big explanation as to why he disappeared. At this point, all I desired to know was that he was okay.

After a week of being down in the dumps, I decided to pick myself back up and get back to the old Terri. The Terri that I was before I had fallen head over hills in love. I went back to work and resumed my old life and while I wished Carlos was still a part of it, I found comfort in doing things the way I used to do them. One day I came home from work and grabbed my mail like I always do. Once I got settled in, I looked through the stack of mail that contained bills, credit card statements, and catalogs and at the end of the stack there was a letter without a return address that was addressed to me:

> *Terri,*
>
> *I know that you don't know me, but I'm Cinthia, Carlos' mom. I know you've been wondering where he has been, and he told me to write you and to tell you to come and visit me so he can tell you in person just what's been going on. If you have any questions, please don't hesitate to call me and I've enclosed a plane ticket and the address to my home. Hope to hear from you soon.*
>
> *Cinthia*

My heart skipped a beat at the mention of his name. It didn't take me any time to grab my *Louis Vuitton* duffel bag, pack some clothes, grab my phone charger and hop back in my BMW to head straight for the airport. I called Denise while I was driving to the airport to let her know I was going to Texas to see Carlos. She told me to be careful and to call her when I found out what was going on. I didn't call my mother until I landed at the *George Bush Intercontinental Airport* in Houston.

"Hey mom, don't be concerned, but I just landed in Houston."

"I didn't know you were going to Houston."

"Apparently, I didn't know I was going either until I got home from work earlier today when I received a note from Carlos' mother. She gave me a plane ticket and her address and said that Carlos wants to talk to me in person."

Jessica A. Robinson

"Well, I'm glad you finally heard something. I was starting to get worried about you and him."

"I'm glad I heard something too, but I'm still worried Mom."

"I know you are still worried Terri, but I've been praying about it and I know everything will be okay. Please call me when you get to where you're going."

"I will. I'll talk to you later." I said as I hung up the phone. I surely hoped my mother was telling the truth.

After I retrieved my luggage from the baggage claim, I took a cab to the address that was listed in the letter and I arrived in front of a beautiful, two-story home that had the most beautiful landscaping in the front yard. From the looks of it, you could tell that Carlos had a hand in designing the house because at first glance it was absolutely breathtaking. I paid the cab driver, gave him a tip, and then I put my duffel bag on my shoulder. I walked up the sidewalk, then up the steps and finally, I knocked on the door. It wasn't long before someone came to the door. I had never seen a picture of his mother, but I could surely tell the Puerto-Rican woman standing before me was his mother because Carlos looked exactly like her.

"Hi, my name is Terri. Are you Cinthia?" I asked.

"Yes, I'm Carlos' mom. It's so nice to finally meet you, please come in." She said, as I walked through the door and into the living room where there was a woman sitting on the couch.

"Terri this is my daughter, Amanda" Cinthia said, as Amanda walked over to me and gave me a hug. She was short with long black curly hair. She and Carlos resembled each other so much.

"We're so glad you came. And I know my brother is happy you came as well."

"So, what's going on? Where's Carlos?" I asked as his mother motioned for me to sit down.

HOLY REVENGE

"Well, there's a lot that you need to find out, and we would love to tell you, but Carlos made us promise not to tell you anything. He said he wants to tell you in person."

"Well, where is he?"

Cinthia looked at Amanda and then they both turned to look at me.

"He's in prison and we can't visit him until tomorrow." Amanda answered, as my mind began to race once again. I had to prepare myself for one of the longest nights of my life because I still didn't know what was going on with Carlos and I was staying in a house filled with people that knew exactly what was going on, but weren't planning on telling me anything. All I knew was Carlos was in prison and I didn't have the slightest clue as to why.

Chapter 20 (Denise)

"I've missed being with you." Randy whispered into my ear as he held me from behind.

"Me too. I've missed you too." I answered, as I rolled my eyes. I was glad he was behind me and not in front of me because he would've definitely been able to tell that I was pissed off. Randy kissed the back of my shoulder, the nape of my neck, and then pulled me in closer to him.

"I've missed the smell of your hair, the scent of your skin, and the way your body feels next to mine."

I wanted to open up my mouth and tell him that there were things I missed too. I missed how he *used* to put it down in the bedroom and the way he *used* to make me feel when we were having sex. But I didn't feel like getting into an argument, so I just kept those comments to myself.

This was the sixth time we'd had sex in the past few days and it was bad to say the least. I was used to a certain level of satisfaction with my husband, and I don't know what the heck that was. Maybe Randy had put me on a sex strike for too long and lost his skills during the time off. I don't know for sure what happened, but whatever it was, I was not satisfied at all.

"I'm just glad that we are no longer fighting with each other and we're able to move past all that." I managed to say without sounding irritated.

"I hate fighting with you too baby." Randy replied. I slid my body away from his and put my silk kimono on as I got out of the bed.

"With loving as good as this, you make me not want to go into church today so I can stay home in your arms, but I know I have work to do."

I know Randy must be joking. He can't possibly think that what we just did was good. Maybe he wasn't used to being with me in so long that what we did felt good to him, but that was far from what I was feeling.

Randy glanced over at the alarm clock and then hopped out of bed.

"Babe, it's almost nine and I have to meet someone at the church at nine forty five. I better hurry up and get ready. Would you like to join me for a shower?" He asked as he stood in the bathroom door.

"No, I better not or you'll be late for work and we both know that won't be good." I laughed.

"You're absolutely right." Randy blew me an air kiss and then went to take a shower. I laid there while he showered trying to figure out how I was going to see Kenny again when I received a text message from him.

Denise,

I know you said you didn't know when we were going to have a chance to see each other again, but come and see me this morning. I called in sick today. Come and be sick with me. ;-)

I smiled and laughed at the fact that he was able to read my mind from all the way across town. I typed back:

See you soon...

When Randy came out of the bathroom, I let him know that I would be late coming down to the church. I told him I had some errands to run and he was fine with that, which gave me all the time in the world to go and pay Kenny a visit.

"This is just what I needed." I said as I lay intertwined with Kenny's body.

"Apparently, it's what the doctor ordered for me too because I'm feeling better already." Kenny smiled and I started to laugh.

Jessica A. Robinson

"Oh, shut up, you weren't even sick." I teased.

"I know, but if I so happened to be under the weather you would have to be my cure." He replied and then he said, "So tell me."

"Tell you what?"

"If you're not happy in your marriage then why do you stay?" He asked me.

"I never said that I was unhappy." I corrected him.

"Come on Denise, you don't have to say it. Your actions speak way louder than you ever could. I see it in your eyes when I look at you. I see it in your step when you walk. You're not happy."

"Whatever Kenny. You don't know what you're talking about." I replied. Who did Kenny think he was—my therapist? Did he think he was Dr. Phil or something?

"You may not want to admit it, but I know that you're not happy and it's cool...you can be in denial if you want to."

I didn't appreciate Kenny trying to diagnose what my problem was, even though he was pretty much on point. He was right. I wasn't happy. And with the way I was feeling, I was headed toward a dangerous place that even I didn't know how to avoid.

I pulled in the parking lot of the church close to noon, extremely exhausted from all of the sexual escapades Kenny and I participated in for most of the morning. I was still able to pull my appearance together, and before I arrived at the church I stopped off and grabbed me an energy drink from the gas station at the corner. When I got inside, I went straight to my husband's office. He was on the phone with someone wrapping up his conversation. He smiled at me as I sat down on the couch. When he ended his call he came over and joined me.

"Hey honey, did you get everything you needed done?" He asked as he gave me a quick kiss on my lips.

HOLY REVENGE

"I sure did babe. How are things here at the church? Are you all caught up for the day?"

"For the most part. Kenny called off sick this morning so until you came, I was answering all the calls that came into the church, which is not my favorite thing to do, but it must be done."

"Well, don't worry about doing that anymore. I'll just go to my office and filter all the calls to my line." I replied.

"Thank you so much baby." He answered.

I was getting ready to say something else when there was a few knocks at the door and in walked Myra. I rolled my eyes and stared at her.

"Hey Pastor, I'm so sorry. I didn't mean to barge into your office. I hope I'm not disturbing anything." Myra apologized. I got up from where I was standing and picked my *Red Hermes Birkin* bag up off the coffee table.

"Well, even if you were disturbing something. We're finished. Honey if you need me I'll be in my office." I turned toward my husband and then I walked out and went down the hallway to my office and away from Myra. I don't know what it was about Myra Washington, but her very presence irritated me and I could barely stand to be around her.

Ever since she accepted the associate minister position a few weeks ago, she's been a literal pain in my side, and I was doing the best I could to try and respect her, but my patience was wearing thin. She had become another issue in our mounting list of problems that we fought over, so I did the best I could not to let her make me upset, but today she was definitely trying me.

I unlocked the door to my office and sat my things down and then called my mother to check on Kaylah.

"Hey mom, so how are you doing with Kaylah?" I asked as I logged into my computer and then logged onto the Internet.

"I'm lovin' the fact that she's here with me and your stepdad. I know that we're supposed to bring her back in two days, but do you mind if we keep her for another week?" My mother asked.

"I miss her, but that's fine, you can keep her for another week. It feels good to have this break. Do you need me to send anything for her?"

"No, don't worry about it. We've been shopping and brought her a lot of things, so she has everything she needs. So you and Randy take this time and enjoy each other."

"We'll try." I told my mother. When she had first agreed to keep Kaylah for two weeks, I had told her about what was going on between us and she prayed with me and encouraged me. She told me that things would get better, and while they weren't perfect, they were definitely improving from what they had been.

"How are things between you two?" My mother asked.

"They've been kind of rough mom, I'm not even going to lie, but as of a few days ago things started getting better."

"Well, I'm glad to hear that. Marriage is hard work Denise, as long as both of you two are willing to sacrifice and do what it takes to make things work, it will."

"I understand, and that's what we're trying to do. I'm just glad that the man you were messing with is no longer in the way of you and Randy working things out. And while I would never wish death on anyone, God knew what he was doing."

"I agree. Well, Mom I gotta go, but kiss my baby for me, and if you need me to send anything for her just let me know. And tell dad I said, 'hello." I said as we exchanged an 'I love you' and hung up. My mother was praising God because the roadblock that was standing in between Randy and I had been eliminated, but little did she know, someone else had just stepped up and created yet another road.

HOLY REVENGE

I was happy though that she volunteered to keep Kaylah for another week because I could surely use the vacation. I loved being a mother, and wouldn't trade it for anything in this world; but it was nothing like having a little free time. Grandparents were a true blessing from God, and I was glad that my daughter had two sets. I logged into my *Yahoo* email account and saw that I had an unread chat message so I clicked the box open.

> *Anonymous: If I were you, I would stop doing what I was doing unless you want to die!*
> *Me: Who is this?*
> *Anonymous: Don't be concerned with who I am. Be concerned with what you're still doing.*
> *Me: Just leave me alone. You don't know what you're talking about.*
> *Anonymous: I know exactly what I'm talking about, and if you don't stop what you're doing, everyone will know!*

I clicked off the message and logged out of my computer altogether. If the disturbing phone calls, being followed, and my car being totally vandalized wasn't enough; now they wanted to send me anonymous email messages too. Even though I had tried for as long as I could to play it all off like I wasn't concerned, things were starting to bother me and I had to tell Randy about everything. Once and for all.

I got up and started to walk out of my office when Myra walked up to me and asked could she come in for a second.

"I was just getting ready to step out for a second but that's okay. It seems like you have a real knack for always disturbing things." I replied as I turned back around and took a seat at my desk.

"I wasn't sure that coming in here to talk to you would be a good idea, but now I see that it is definitely needed. I wanted to come and talk to you so we could attempt to straighten some things out." Myra said as she sat in one of the chairs in front of my desk.

"Straighten what out, what are you talking about?" I asked as I played like I was clueless.

"Come on Denise, you can sit here and play around like you don't know what I'm talking about, but ever since I've come on staff you seem as though you have an attitude with me."

I laughed at her accusation.

"An attitude with you? Come on, don't be serious. I haven't had, nor do I have, an attitude with you Myra." I replied even though I knew she was telling the truth.

"Okay, I see this is going to be harder than I thought. I understand that you're trying to tell me that you haven't been acting funny since I've come here, but I know what I feel in my spirit, and also what I see first-hand. Are you acting this way because you think I want your husband?" Myra asked me.

"I'm not sure. You tell me." I was interested in hearing her answer.

"If you think that I wanted to come here because I want your husband then you're wrong. I'm on an assignment from God and it has nothing to do with your husband. Now, don't get me wrong, your husband is a very attractive man, but that is neither my aim, nor my mission. I came to be a part of this ministry because the Lord led me here, not because of a man so you can rest assured that my heart and motives are in the right place." She reassured me.

"Well, that's good to know." I answered not knowing what else to say.

"I'm glad we had this talk. Have a good day first lady." Myra said and walked out of my office leaving me even more pissed off than I already was.

HOLY REVENGE

Chapter 21 (Terri)

The waiting area in the county jail was packed full of people who were waiting to see someone. Me, Cinthia, and Amanda found the only available seats after signing in, and we didn't have to wait long before they called us. I got up from where I was sitting and thought Cinthia and Amanda were going to come with me, but they remained in their seats.

"Are you coming with me?" I asked as I stopped walking and looked back at them.

"No, honey, go ahead. We've already talked to Carlos. We want you to have time alone so you two can talk." Cinthia said as she stood up and gave me a hug and then I followed the female officer through a door and then down a long hallway, into a room where she asked me to have a seat.

I sat there for about five minutes before five inmates were escorted in the room and sat at separate tables where their family and friends were. Carlos was the last person to be brought in. Everything within me wanted to bum rush him and shower him with a million kisses because he was okay. But there was another part of me that remained cool and unaffected as I waited for him to sit down. My face was blank and my emotions were hidden. I needed Carlos to give me some real answers so everything would make sense.

He smiled, as he sat across from me and I pressed my lips together and gave him the best smile that I could.

"I'm so glad you came. I thought you might not come at all."

"Why would you think that?" I asked.

"Because you haven't heard from me in two weeks and I thought you might be too mad to come, but my sister suggested instead of calling you to tell you what was going on, that I should just send you a letter and a plane ticket because it was better said in person."

"Well, I'm here and I'm listening." I replied as I folded my hands together on top of the table.

Carlos took deep breath and then proceeded to tell me everything.

"I know what I'm about to tell you is going to shock you, but I have to come clean and tell you everything. I used to be married a few years ago to a woman named Estella and we have a daughter named Lilly. While I was married I had a bad problem with drinking. I used to be drunk more than I was sober. Estella and I used to argue all the time, and some of our disagreements even turned physical. My alcohol problem resulted in us getting a divorce.

After we divorced, I ended up going to a treatment center and I turned my life around and started my own business. Even though I had completely changed my life, Estella and I still didn't get along and it became too much to deal with. To avoid all the arguments, I took my company and moved to Ohio. But Estella continued to harass me and when she found out that I was dating you, she started trying to blackmail me and that's how I ended up here." Carlos explained.

So I had finally figured out who Estella was. She was the one who had probably called him and got him all upset and she definitely was the woman who called me trying to warn me. Now, it was all coming together.

"So, why didn't you tell me any of this? Carlos we've been dating for almost a year, and you mean to tell me you never felt the need to tell me any of this."

"Yes, I was planning to tell you, but I just didn't want to have to tell you like this. Terri, I'm sorry that I wasn't totally honest with you, but I was afraid that you wouldn't want to be with me if you found out about my past."

"Why would you think I would do that? I love you Carlos." I said as I grabbed his hands and locked them in between mine.

"And I love you too, but my past is a dark place for me, and I wasn't sure if it would stop you from wanting to be with me. All I know is, I just didn't want to lose you."

"I don't want to lose you either. I can't hold your past against you Carlos. What was done is done. All I care about is now." I replied as I stroked the side of his hand.

"I'm glad to hear that, but now I'm facing a major battle with Estella. She has set a case up against me so strong that it's going to take God himself to get me out."

"Listen to me. Don't worry about how you're going to get out of this mess. We're in this together and we'll figure it out." I replied and then made a mental note to call the one person who I knew could help me and Carlos—my colleague, Winston Christopher. If anyone knew how to pull off a miracle, it would be him, and I surely hoped he could perform a miracle this time.

Chapter 22 (Randy)

"**D**enise I can't believe you're just telling me all of this now. Why did you wait so long to tell me that someone was harassing you?" I asked as Denise sat next to me on the couch. We had just gotten finished eating dinner and she told me she had to talk to me about something.

"Because I didn't want you to worry, like you're doing now. I just wanted to make sure you're aware that this was taking place."

"So, how long has this been going on?" I asked.

"Ever since Tyrone's funeral. I've been getting phone calls, text messages, and emails and one time I even believe I was being followed."

"And you just never thought enough about it to tell me or what?"

"Well, at first I thought that it was just people trying to be funny and hating on me, but the more and more it kept happening, it made me start to get nervous. And the message I received today topped it all. The person even threatened to kill me."

"Do you have any of the messages that they sent you?" I asked.

"No, I've erased them. I didn't really think about them all until now."

"See now it's going to be hard to prove that you've received anything. If anyone else calls or texts you please save it so we can trace where it's coming from."

"Okay, I will."

"And until we figure this out, I don't want you to go anywhere by yourself. I'm actually glad the baby is with your mom."

"Me too. I'm just nervous baby. What if the person is following me? Following us?"

"Listen, God has not given us the spirit of fear, but of love, power, and a sound mind. We're not going to live in fear at all. What we're going to do is pray and continue to live our lives, but I do want us to take the proper precautions and be safe about everything."

"I agree honey. I'm not going to be afraid. I'm going to just pray like you said."

Denise yawned and rubbed her eyes. "Baby, I don't mean to go to bed all early, but I've had a really long day and I think I'm going to turn in a little early."

"That's fine. You go up and get you some rest. I'll be joining you shortly." I replied as I gave my wife a big hug and kissed her before she walked up the steps. I went down the hall to my study and briefly turned on *ESPN* to catch up on watching *Sports Center* when I felt the sudden urge to pray. I turned my T.V. off and then I got down on my knees. It disturbed me to hear that my wife had been harassed and bothered for months. I was even more nervous to think that she had to endure these things while our daughter was with her. I don't know what I would do if something happened to her or Kaylah. For some reason, I felt like although Denise had told me most of what was going on, she wasn't telling me the complete truth. The only thing I felt I could do right now was pray, so I bowed my head and closed my eyes in prayer.

Lord,
Right now I come to you the best way I know how. I'm asking that you intervene in this situation right now. I pray that you would keep my wife and daughter safe; and that the people that have been bothering her—I pray that it comes to an end. You said in your Word that God has

not given us a spirit of fear, and I pray that we won't be afraid to live our lives, but that you would protect us and guide our steps each and every day. I ask all these things in Jesus name, Amen.

The next morning, I got dressed and went down to the church to start my normal routine. Denise decided to stay home from the church, which was fine with me, because our maid, Marisol, was there and she would at least have company until I got home.

"Hey Kenny. It's good to see you this morning. How are you feeling?" I asked as I walked into the building and saw Kenny sitting in his chair.

"Oh, I'm feeling much better. I think I had a little stomach flu, but the doctor gave me just what I needed and now I'm feeling much better."

"That's good to hear. I'm glad you're doing okay. If you need me, I'll be in my office." I replied as I walked down the hall to my office.

I looked through a stack of bills and invitations to speak at several events; then I checked my voicemail.

The first message was from my little brother:
Hey Bro. I just received letters from the University of North Carolina and Georgetown University and they are excited about meeting with me and giving me a tour of their campus. I didn't know how dad was going to take it, but after we sat down and had a heart to heart, he finally saw things my way, and while he's not jumping up and down because I decided not to attend the seminary, he said if I promised to hook him and mom up with season tickets; then we can call it even. There's more to tell you, but I want to share that with you in person. Call me later. Love ya.

HOLY REVENGE

I smiled as I listened to Will's message. I hadn't gotten a chance to actually talk to my dad about Will going to college on a basketball scholarship, but I see that God was already working it out. I was excited that he stuck to his guns and was adamant about wanting to pursue his college basketball career. I was a firm believer that not everyone's ministry was from the pulpit, and God could use my brother mightily through his talents and gifts.

My next voicemail was from Alexis:

Hey, Junior, or should I say Pastor...I was just calling to tell you that I've gotten back to Atlanta and got settled and everything. Even though Teddy is trying to tarnish my name, I'm still encouraged and I just want to thank you for always being there. I'll give you a call in a few days and keep you updated. Talk to you soon.

I was so glad she called me to let me know how she was doing. I had been thinking about her on and off ever since she left for Atlanta last week. It was good to hear her voice and I hoped that things were really working out for her. I knew I would probably call her back before she called me, just to make sure she was okay.

I picked up the stack of bills and a letter addressed to me fell onto my desk. It had no return address and it was written in fancy calligraphy. I opened up the beautiful letter and read it:

Your wife is a little whore and even though you're still in denial, you won't be for very long.

As I sat there and examined the letter, I wondered who had sent it to me, but the handwriting was almost perfect like it had been practiced over and over again. There was no way I could tell who had sent it to me and there wasn't a return address or a signature. I folded the letter back up and put it inside my jacket pocket. Although I tried to shrug the note off like it didn't mean anything, I couldn't help but wonder what I was going to find out *sooner* rather than *later*.

HOLY REVENGE

Chapter 23 (Terri)

"I don't know how you do what you do, but you're good at it." Carlos said as he picked me up and spun me around in a circle. We had just come in from the airport and I was dropping him off at his house.

"You don't have to thank me. Thank my colleague, Winston. His brother is the one who came in and got all of your charges dropped."

"Well, whoever it was, I'm thankful that they stepped in and helped me out because I was facing some major time."

"I'm thankful too."

As soon as I left from seeing Carlos, I called my friend Winston. Just as I suspected, he knew exactly who to call and actually had a brother named Walter who was a lawyer in the Houston area. Once he told him what was going on, Walter wasted no time in taking over the case and in three days Carlos walked out of jail a free man. Even though Estella had tried to build up a case against him, Walter found all the loopholes in her story, and she ended up looking like a complete idiot in court. It didn't take a blind man to see that she was lying, and Carlos was free because of it.

Walter had even fixed it so that Carlos could see his daughter, Lilly, who he hadn't seen in almost three years. Now he has visitation, and has a chance to get her on every other holiday and for the summer too. He's a great father from what I can see, and even though I was initially pissed because I didn't know that he was married or had a daughter, I'm not mad anymore. I understand why he didn't tell me everything in the beginning, and I'm fine with that.

"I don't know how I will ever repay you for all you've done for me Terri. I owe you my life." Carlos said as he pulled the last of his luggage into the house.

"You don't have to repay me. All I want you to do is continue to love me like you're doing. I didn't just do that for you, I did that for us." I smiled and then Carlos took me by the hand.

"And that's what I love about you. Most women wouldn't have understood or even cared about my situation, but not you. You stepped in at a time when I needed you most, and you're still here by my side. You're a good woman. My mother always told me when I came across a good woman to hold on to her, and I don't plan on letting you go. You're the best thing that has ever happened to me and I don't want to live without you." Carlos said.

"I don't plan on letting you go either." I answered. Then Carlos got down on one knee and reached inside his pocket. He pulled out a light blue box with a white bow and asked, "Terri will you make me the happiest man on earth and marry me?" He opened the box to reveal one of the biggest diamond solitaire rings I'd ever seen.

"Yes, Carlos! Yes, I'll marry you!" I replied, as he slid the huge rock on my finger and then picked me up in his arms. This had to be the happiest day of my life.

Chapter 24 (Denise)

I knew Randy was going to freak out when I told him about all of the things I've been going through for the past couple months, but I couldn't take it anymore. I was starting to get scared that there was really somebody out there who was trying to hurt me, and I felt it was better that he was aware of everything that was going on. The entire day I sat home and tried to come up with who might be trying to harass me, but I couldn't think of anyone. The only person who I thought would come close to wanting to cause me harm was Jackson's wife, and I doubted it was her.

Besides, after I got my test results showing that I was positive for Chlamydia, I paid Jackson a little visit. Of course he was in denial about being the one to give it to me and told me to leave his office at once, and that was fine with me. Since he was so generous and left me with such a horrible disease, I decided to leave him with a present of my own.

Before I left the parking lot, I pulled out a spray can of black paint and decorated his Bentley GT with the phrase, "Don't talk to me I have an STD." Just in case he missed that phrase which was on the hood of his car, I spray painted all of his windows with the word, "Dirty." I haven't heard from him since, and I don't care to hear from him.

"Denise I'm about to leave for the day, but I just want you to know that I finished the three loads of clothes that needed to be done. Everything's put away, and I even cooked you guys some baked chicken and brown rice and gravy." Marisol said as she grabbed her purse and retrieved her car keys.

"Marisol, you're the absolute best. That is great!" I replied as I gave her a hug and then she walked out of the house. I went into the living room and turned on *BET* and they just so happened to be having a marathon of *The Game* on so I left it there and watched a few episodes while I waited for my husband to come home. After I watched about three episodes, I realized that Randy still hadn't come home yet, so I ran up the steps to grab my phone to see if he called me, but when I pulled my *Blackberry* off the charger, there were no messages or missed calls. I dialed his number and it went straight to voicemail so I left him a message.

> *Hey Baby, it's me. I was wondering where you were. I'm waiting on you to come home. Dinner is ready, all I have to do is heat everything up, thanks to Marisol. See you soon. I love you.*

I pressed the end button on my phone and then I heard the garage door opening so I jogged the steps to greet Randy when he walked through the door, but he never did. I know that I heard the garage door open and I wasn't imagining things. Maybe Randy was getting something out of his truck and that's why he didn't come in yet. I walked through the kitchen and opened the garage door hoping to see Randy, but instead I was met with a blunt force of something hitting me on the back of my head and my back. I tried to look up and see what was going on, but when I tried everything turned to black.

Chapter 25 (Denise)

When I finally woke up, I was sitting in the middle of the sanctuary tied to a chair. My mouth was also taped shut with duct tape. I was bleeding from somewhere on my head, but I didn't know exactly where it was coming from. All I could see was blood dripping on my *True Religion* jeans. Sweat mixed with my own tears and blood clouded my vision and made it difficult to see. I squinted several times until I realized it didn't help me to see any better. I looked around the church to see if I saw anyone, and there was no one in sight. I attempted to wiggle and squirm to try and work myself loose, but to no avail. It seemed like the more I continued to move, the tighter my restraints became.

Since I couldn't move, I decided to make as much noise as I could. I couldn't scream due to the duct tape, so I grunted and moaned as loud as I possibly could. Maybe someone was in the church that could help me, or better yet maybe Randy would realize I was missing and try to come looking for me. It really didn't matter at this point. All I cared about was someone discovering that I was there and clearly in danger.

"What do you think you're doing?" A voice from behind me called out as the sanctuary doors suddenly opened. I still couldn't see who the voice belonged to because I couldn't turn around, but one thing I did know was that the voice sounded so familiar to me.

"I thought I knocked you out good, but I was obviously wrong, you're a resilient lil whore aren't you?" The person said as they walked down the aisle into the light finally revealing who she was.

It was Myra! Since I couldn't speak, my eyes grew wide and they honestly felt like they were going to pop out of their sockets.

"I bet you're surprised to see me huh? Are you surprised? If looks could kill I'd be a millionaire right now." She smirked as she moved closer to me. I sort of flinched because I didn't know what she was about to do to me. She reached for the duct tape that was covering my mouth and ripped it off. The sensation of it being pulled from my lips hurt so bad and caused me to scream out in pain.

"Myra, what are you doing?" I simply asked.

"AH, AH, AH...now is not the time for you to be asking any questions that's my job. But it is your job to figure out why you're here." Myra explained.

"I don't have a clue why I'm here." I replied.

"See, I had a feeling you were going to play the clueless role...and by the way, you're good at it. Since you're having some difficulty in this area, I'm going to help you figure it all out, but hold on, I have someone special here for you because I don't want them to miss a thing." Myra reached behind her back and pulled a .45mm handgun. She walked back up the aisle opened the door and then pushed Randy inside and walked with him down the aisle until he was standing next to me.

"Randy...Oh, my God baby, are you okay?" I asked as she ordered him to sit in a chair that was next to me.

"I'm fine Denise. I'm just glad to see you're still alive." He answered.

"Shut up! Did I ask you two to talk? I'm running this show, and if I don't give you permission, then you better not speak. If you don't understand what 'shut up' means, then I can always shut you up." Myra waved the gun back and forth and caused our conversation to be cut short.

"Okay, now that we all have an understanding, let's get this party started. I never really knew that I actually had talent as a filmmaker until I put this small feature together.   I am so surprised because it is actually fabulous, and will definitely leave you with your mouths hanging wide open. So without further ado, I present to you my first feature film, the *Holy Whore*." She pushed the button on the remote which caused the screen to come down from the ceiling and then she pressed *Start*.

Randy and I looked on as images of me continuously popped on the screen. There were photographs of me going to Darnell's house, us at the park with Kaylah, pictures of me and Jackson, pictures of me and Kenny, and if that wasn't bad enough the last part of her, "so-called" movie contained footage of Kenny and I having sex on a few different occasions.

After Myra pressed the *Stop* button, all I could do was look down and cry. I cried because no matter how I could try to deny all of the allegations, the proof was in the pudding. I was caught red handed cheating on my husband. The very thing I had tried so hard not to do, but failed horribly at. I couldn't even look up at all. I was too embarrassed.

She began to clap like she had just finished watching a *Tyler Perry* movie.

"Denise you're a star! I must admit, I didn't know you had it in you."

"You're sick Myra, you know that?" I said. Now, I know that wasn't the smartest thing to say to her at the moment, but I felt like if I was getting ready to die then I might as well speak my mind to some degree.

"I'm sick? You're the one that's sick—having sex with all those men and then going home and screwing your husband at night. You're nasty Denise, but here I go getting ahead of myself. I almost forgot I have another special person to bring out."

"Who?" I asked in a confused tone.

Myra cleared her throat and then raised her voice like she was an announcer.

HOLY REVENGE

"You saw him in *Holy Whore* which was his debut performance, now I would like to introduce to you the main man of this whole feature...Kenny!" She turned her attention to the side door and in walked Kenny. I swear I almost peed on myself. He walked in smiling from ear to ear like he had just won the *Mega Million*.

"Thank you so much for this opportunity Myra...I appreciate it so much, and honestly, I didn't think I could do justice to this role, but with God and your guidance, I figured out I was a natural." He smiled and then winked at me. I felt instantly sick when he looked over at me. His very presence made me sick to my stomach.

"Kenny what's going on?" I asked. I was still completely clueless and still couldn't put two and two together.

"I'll tell you what's going on. You're finally being found out for the trifling hoe that you are." Kenny said as he looked at me as though he were disgusted.

"Why are you doing this? Myra you don't even know me." I replied.

"See that's where you're wrong again Denise. You may not know me, but I know you very well. Tyrone—God rest his soul—couldn't stop talking about you. He was in love with you, and thought that you would be his wife one day. I actually thought you were going to be my sister-in-law one day. I never even thought that you would play my brother the way you did." She replied.

"Oh, my God, Tyrone was your brother?" I asked.

"That would be right. Tyrone was my brother and the only somebody that cared about me in this world and you took him away from me. You caused him to go crazy and to flip out, all because you were selfish and didn't want to be honest with him.

You should've just left my brother alone but, 'no'...you insisted on continuing a relationship with him when you knew that you never were gonna leave. I'll never forgive you for what you did to me. You took away my brother, and you took away Kenny's best friend. I hate you, that's why I took it upon myself to come here just so that I could take pleasure in killing you myself." Myra answered as she aimed the gun directly in my face. I couldn't believe that Myra was Tyrone's sister and Kenny was his best friend. I never saw that coming at all.

"Myra you think that killing Denise will solve everything? I'm telling you it won't. Please put the gun down. She's not even worth it. So please put the gun down so we can all talk about this." Randy said as he turned to address Myra. I started to get offended at what he said, but I figured since we were in a desperate situation, he had to do what was best. I remained silent and just prayed to myself. I know I had a lot of nerve, but I prayed that if God would just help me get through this situation that I would change my wicked ways once and for all.

Momentarily, Myra's concentration on me was broken and she turned to face Randy.

"Pastor Randy, I know you're only trying to help, but this has nothing to do with you. You're a really great man and I believe that God has really called you into the ministry, but you really need to do extensive background checks on who you allow to be hired at your church next time. If your search on the Internet was a little more thorough you would've discovered that I received my ministerial certificate online at one of those sites where you pay for it, and I posted a few videos of some events that I was allowed to speak at. Bottom line is I created myself to be a minister with the sole purpose of attracting your attention, so that I could get closer to her. I'm sorry that you're even involved, but you can't stop what's about to happen. I've been waiting to do this for a very long time and I don't intend on hurting you, but I will if you try to stand in my way." Myra warned.

HOLY REVENGE

"I hate you and I can't wait to see you take your last breath. This is the moment I've been waiting for." Myra raised the gun to my head and then laughed as she pulled the trigger and ended my life just like that.

Chapter 26 (Randy)

The hospital called to inform me that Denise had finally awakened from the coma that she had been in since she'd been shot. I must admit, I didn't even feel like going up there to see her at all, but I guess the compassionate, pastor-like side of me took over because no sooner than I had hung up the phone with the Intensive Care Nurse, I was getting in my car and making my way to *St. Elizabeth Hospital.*

Sometimes I wish my heart wasn't as caring as it is, but I was that way because of the calling God had placed on my life, and there was absolutely nothing I could do to change that. Don't get me wrong; everything within me right now wants to say, 'to hell' with Denise and everything associated with her, but I know that's the wrong way to be.

As I drove to the hospital in silence, there had to be a million and one thoughts swimming around in my head and even more emotions that I was feeling. I wanted to see her, but I wasn't sure of what I wanted to say to her. I said a short prayer, and asked God to direct my steps and to help me to say the right things. I parked my car in the parking deck, took the walkway directly into the hospital and went up four floors on the elevator to the Intensive Care Unit where Denise was.

The closer I got to her room, the more nervous I became. My hands were shaky, my palms were sweaty, and my mouth was extremely dry. Thank God there was a water fountain close by. I stopped to take a short sip, and then I walked down the hallway to room 4402—my wife's private room. The door was slightly ajar, and the room appeared to be quiet which meant she probably didn't have any visitors, which wasn't a bad thing because this was definitely a moment where we needed to be alone.

Before I walked in her room, a tall brunette woman, who appeared to be a nurse, grabbed my arm.

"Excuse me sir, are you Randy Tate?" She asked.

"Yes, that's me. Why?" I asked her.

She seemed to breathe a sigh of relief and smiled at me.

"Well, ever since she woke up you're the only person she's been asking to see besides her daughter. I honestly didn't know when you were coming, but I've been telling her you would be here soon. I'm just glad you actually made it."

"Okay...is it okay if I go in and see her?"

"Sure, if you need anything at all, I'll be right down the hallway at the nurse's station."

"Thank you so much." I replied and watched the tall, lanky, nurse disappear down the hallway. I took a deep breath, exhaled, and then pressed the heavy wooden door open. I tried to be as quiet as I could, but when I tried to pull the door shut it slammed instead. The loud, sudden noise woke Denise up from her sleep.

"Randy you're here. I didn't think you would come." She said as she attempted to sit up in her bed, but all she could do was grimace in pain.

My mind flashed back to the day that landed her in the hospital. When Myra shot Denise, she initially aimed to hit her directly in her head, but with the force of the gun being so great, she ended up hitting her in the chest, only a few inches from piercing her heart. The hand of God had spared her once again and it was truly a miracle she wasn't dead.

After Myra shot Denise, I tackled her to the ground and wrestled with her until I got the gun away from her. Once I picked up the gun I held Myra hostage until the authorities came. As for Kenny, he fled as soon as Myra fired the gun. I wondered why he left so suddenly, but I later found out that he had been in some previous trouble with the law and escaped without having to serve any jail time. He knew that if he was around when the police came he would never see the light of day again. He left the church and apparently the city because I never seen or heard from him again.

"Well, the nurse called me a few hours ago and told me you finally woke up, so I told her I would be on my way." I answered her and sat in the chair that was next to the bed. When I sat down, I tried to come up with the words that I wanted to say to her that would jumpstart our conversation, but my mind went completely blank. All I could do was look at her and she looked back at me just as speechless as I was.

She reached out for my hand. Even though holding her hand was the last thing I wanted to do at this point, she was still my wife, the woman I cared for, and she had come so close to death that the least I could do was offer her some moral support. I grabbed her hand and held it in between my hands. She began to cry almost immediately. Tears began to fall and run down her bruised and battered face. Seeing her cry threw me off because I had never seen her cry at all. I didn't know what to think or say. I just remained quiet and rubbed her hand.

"I'm so sorry..." Denise said, as she paused to try to get herself together, but was too overcome with emotion to gain any type of composure.

"You've been such a good man and husband to me and all I've done is treated you bad. I've done you wrong. I feel so horrible and I know I'm such a bad person and you've experienced so many crazy things since I've been in your life. I don't know how I'll ever be able to forgive myself. I just don't know what else to say, other than, 'I'm sorry' and although I know you must really hate me right now, I pray that you can find it in your heart to forgive me and hopefully we can make it past all of this and still be together. I love you

HOLY REVENGE

from the bottom of my heart Randy, and I'm sorry…I'm just so sorry." She began to cry all over again.

Okay, Denise must be extremely high off of her pain meds. Her little, Hollywood monologue she just recited didn't move me at all. The sad part is, I know she's being sincere, but sometimes that just isn't good enough.

"You know I've been doing a lot of thinking and praying over the past few days trying to figure out what I was going to say to you, or how I was going to respond to what you were going to say, and never in a million years did I ever picture you saying something like that. I can't believe you have the audacity to sit there and ask me to see past all of this so we can still be together. Denise, I've been nothing but a good man to you since day one, but you've taken my goodness and kindness for weakness. I've tried sticking by you through the thick and thin, good and the bad, but it comes to a point where I stop playing the fool. I did what I was supposed to do as a man, so at least I can walk away with my head held high knowing I tried."

"No! Don't say that…don't walk away from me, I need you. I love you baby." Denise pleaded as she began to sob.

"You don't *need* me Denise. Well, maybe you need my money, my status and my lifestyle; but let's both be honest…you definitely don't need me. I know you may have love for me, but you're not *in love* with anyone but yourself. I think you need to be alone so that you can do exactly what you want to do, and I'm going to give you the opportunity to do just that."

"So you're divorcing me? Denise asked.

I took a deep breath before I answered her.

"Yes, I'm divorcing you. Just like you need to be free, I need the same freedom so that God can bring the right woman my way who truly loves me. I'm not going to pretend anymore, and I'm definitely not going to try and hold on to something that is potentially stopping me from truly being blessed." I said as I got up from the chair in which I was sitting and was getting ready to leave, when her whole entire attitude shifted.

"So you're just going to leave me and Kaylah like that? And you're gonna sit up here and talk about *I don't love you*, you're the one who doesn't love me...probably never did."

I was wondering when the *real* Denise was going to show up.

I actually couldn't believe what I was hearing. After all that woman has put me through, she has the nerve of accusing *my* love of not being real? I'm sad to say this, but I knew she would respond this way, which is why I tried to avoid conflict with her at all cost, but this dispute right here—she brought entirely on herself.

"I never loved you? You actually believe that bogus statement? So if I never loved you, then your love for me must be more authentic than the mink coat you have sitting at home. I have a hard time believing the fact that you actually *loved me* when you practically screwed every man in this city. So before you accuse me of *not* loving you, I think you need to check yourself, because you seem to have it all twisted." I replied.

From the look on her face, I could tell I hit a nerve. I really hit home with that statement, but I didn't care too much at that point. I was way past caring about her feelings.

"Oh, I see someone is very quiet now, so again, I say, *I don't love you*? I've even stepped in and been a stand up man and raised a daughter that's not even mine, paying people off, and keeping this big old secret, all because you'd rather live a lie, than tell the complete truth. So if that isn't love, then I don't know what is.

I've done my part and been there for you like no one else has, so as far as I'm concerned, none of this is on my hands anymore. I could choose to sit here and argue with you trying to avoid the inevitable, but that's not the choice I'm making. Goodbye Denise." I replied and then shut the door to her room before she even had

HOLY REVENGE

the chance to speak again. I was completely through with Denise and her excuses. Now it was time to live my life in a fresh new way.

I walked down the hallway and pressed the elevator button to go back down toward the direction of my car. I got in my SUV and drove to my parent's house. I could've gone home, but I really didn't feel like being there alone.

My mother must've anticipated my visit, because she was sitting on the porch flipping through an *Essence* magazine when I pulled up.

"Hey mom." I said as I got out of my truck and locked my doors.

"Hey son, I take it you just came from seeing Denise." She said as she motioned for me to sit down next to her.

"Yeah, I just left there. I told her I want a divorce. I'm done." I confessed as I exhaled. It was one thing feeling like I wanted to get a divorce, but actually telling someone else was going to take some getting used to.

"I understand son, and while I'm not an advocate of divorcing your spouse, I can understand why you came to that conclusion. How did she take the news?" My mother asked.

"Now, you know she's not taking it too well, but I can't worry about her. It's time to break free from my relationship with her so I can move on. I mean, I love her and probably always will, but I cannot continue to remain with someone who doesn't love me back."

I thought I was married and *in love* with someone who truly loved me, but what I have truly discovered is that Denise never really loved me in the first place. She may have had *a love* for me, but she wasn't *in love* with me. I think she was in love with the idea of having such a fabulous lifestyle and not having to work, and that's why she claimed to love me—because I provided her with that. But I wasn't concerned about her feelings anymore, now I was going to focus on me.

"So, have you guys said anything about how you're going to raise Kaylah?"

"No, not yet but I'm sure we'll come to some form of agreement after a while." I replied. My mother got up from her chair and walked to the door.

"I have something for you, I'll be right back." She said as she walked in the house.

I didn't know what she had for me, but I hoped it was some food because I was hungry. When she came back out on the porch, she was carrying a Tupperware container with a note on top. She handed it to me and then told me that she had to go check on something she had baking in the oven. The envelope was plain and wasn't addressed to me, but I opened it and there was a letter inside that had my name written at the top. I also removed the top of the container to see it was filled to the brim with my favorite: chocolate chip cookies. They were still fairly warm and by the nature of the scent I knew exactly where the cookies had come from, so I read the letter.

Junior,

I know you're surprised to be hearing from me because I'm supposed to be in Atlanta and I was until my mother called me and told me what had happened at the church. As soon as I called your mom and she told me what was going on, I took the first flight I could and came here. When I landed I was going to drive straight to the hospital to see if you were there, but I decided against it. I decided to make you something that used to make your bad days good. It's something about these chocolate chip cookies that has the ability to cheer you up no matter what.

HOLY REVENGE

I'm so sorry that you had to go through such a horrible thing with your wife, but God always has a way of working things out. I was so nervous to leave Atlanta to come up here, but I just got off the phone with my lawyer and all of the charges have been dropped and my name is cleared from everything, so you see God has a way of making all things work for our good. I'll be moving back here shortly, and while I know you probably don't want to start a relationship with anyone, I know it wasn't mere coincidence that we crossed paths again. I would like to see where things could go from here. When you're ready to talk, just let me know, but in the meantime, enjoy the cookies.
Take care,
Alexis

I looked toward the sky and began to think, *Wow God...Now I know You work in mysterious ways and You are known for doing a quick work, but I never expected for the work to be this fast!*

Well, I guess it isn't up for me to question Him; rather it's my job to just be a servant, and follow Him on this journey called, "life." I stared at her letter for another minute trying to process it all. My life had changed so much practically in an instant, and I couldn't believe everything that had taken place in such a short time.

Alexis was right, although I wasn't nearly ready to date anyone, I was going to prepare myself for the possibilities of what could be. I ate two cookies and then I decided to walk across the grass to personally thank her myself.

Jessica A. Robinson

HOLY REVENGE
DISCUSSION QUESTIONS

1. If your spouse or significant other cheated on you with someone else, would you still be able to remain married to them or would that be immediate grounds for divorce?
2. What is worse: Having an emotional affair or a physical affair with someone and why?
3. Could you accept a child as your own who was conceived as a result of an affair? Or would it be grounds to end the relationship? Why or why not?
4. Do you think it's wrong to keep secrets from your spouse or significant other?
5. Could you love someone who has a dark past?
6. Do you think that Denise really loved Randy?
7. Do you think that something will happen between Alexis and Randy? Why or why not?
8. Who was your favorite character in *Holy Revenge* and why?
9. Did you suspect that anything was wrong with Myra?
10. Did you like the ending? Why or why not?
11. Who would you like to see a book written about next?

PRAISE FOR
HOLY REVENGE

Jessica A. Robinson takes her own drama, 'Church Dramedy,' and blends comedy, drama and the antics of one crazy first lady and creates a phenomenally entertaining reading experience.

~Elissa Gabrielle, President and CEO of Peace In The Storm Publishing

Jessica Robinson reminds us that temptation doesn't discriminate; nor does it care who it takes as a prisoner. Even members of the cloth sometimes stumble and fall to its power. Holy Revenge will keep you on the edge of your seat with anticipation witnessing the unfolding path of vengeance at the hands of what's done in the dark finally coming to light.

~Lorraine Elzia, author of *Ask Nicely and I Might*

Jessica A. Robinson returns First Lady Denise Tate through the side door of her church. Her past sins and temptations, God may have forgiven her—may have, but others don't exempt Denise Tate past behavior, and most transgressions don't sleep alone. Holy Revenge is a nice combination of inner conversations and storytelling.

~Alvin L.A. Horn author of *Brush Strokes* and *Perfect Circle*

HOLY REVENGE

I thought Holy Seduction was drama packed (just like I like it) but it ain't got nothing on Holy Revenge. A must read!
~Allyson M. Deese, author of *Discovering The Joy Within*

PEACE IN THE STORM PUBLISHING, LLC IS THE
WINNER OF THE 2009 & 2010 & 2011 AFRICAN
AMERICAN LITERARY AWARD FOR
INDEPENDENT PUBLISHER OF THE YEAR.

WWW.PEACEINTHESTORMPUBLISHING.COM

MEET
JESSICA A. ROBINSON

JESSICA A. ROBINSON has always had an affinity for reading and creatively expressing herself through written word. Imaginative thoughts soon found a home in personal journals. Journal entries soon became short stories. Short stories gave birth to her first novel. This evolution, which started with creative expression, quickly became her passion.

"Initially, I didn't plan on doing anything with my writing. I wrote short stories because I personally enjoyed creating them; I followed my passion for writing and everything else fell into place."

Jessica feels blessed that something she loves doing has become a craft she can share with the world. Her first novel, *Holy Seduction*, was released in 2009, by *Peace In The Storm Publishing*. With the wind beneath her wings from her debut novel, she penned her second, *Pretty Skeletons*, which was released the following year. *Holy Revenge*, her current release with *Peace In The Storm Publishing*, is a sequel to *Holy Seduction* and allows readers to revisit the woman they love to hate in a Church Dramedy that guarantees to leave you begging for more.

This gifted writer is obedient to her calling of creating stories and situations that readers can relate to. Since the publication of her debut novel, Jessica has won several literary awards and has been featured on *Black Expressions* Top 100 Bestsellers List. Jessica is currently working on her fourth novel entitled, *Between the Pews*, a collaboration with Author Natasha Gooch.

Passions run deep in this young author. Jessica recently became a Registered Nurse, and is also following her dream of providing comfort and care to patients in the Youngstown, Ohio area while pursuing a Bachelor's Degree in Nursing from *Kent State University*.

Jessica A. Robinson